I0654668

Hannah Cowley

A school for Greybeards; or, the Mourning Bride

A Comedy, in Five Acts. As Performed at the Theatre Royal, Drury-Lane

Hannah Cowley

A school for Greybeards; or, the Mourning Bride
A Comedy, in Five Acts. As Performed at the Theatre Royal, Drury-Lane

ISBN/EAN: 9783337002701

Printed in Europe, USA, Canada, Australia, Japan

Cover: Foto ©Andreas Hilbeck / pixelio.de

More available books at **www.hansebooks.com**

A

SCHOOL FOR GREYBEARDS;

OR, THE

MOURNING BRIDE:

A

COMEDY,

IN FIVE ACTS,

AS PERFORMED AT THE

THEATRE ROYAL, DRURY - LANE.

BY MRS. COWLEY,

LONDON:

PRINTED FOR G. G. J. AND J. ROBINSON, PATER-
NOSTER-ROW.

MDCCLXXXVI.

[Price One Shilling and Six-pence.]

A D D R E S S.

I OFFER the following Comedy to the public, under a circumstance which has given my mind the most exquisite uneasiness. On the morning after the first representation, it was observed by the papers that there had been persons present at the Theatre the preceding evening, who went there *determined* to disapprove at all events. From such a determination it is hard indeed to escape! And the opposition intended, was justified it seems, by the indecency of some of the expressions. —From such a charge I feel it impossible to defend myself; for against an imputation like this, even *vindication* becomes disgraceful!

As

As I was not at the Theatre, I fhould have had fome difficulty in underftanding at what paffages the objections were levelled, had not one of the papers recorded them, with many cruel remarks. The particulars which were thus pointed out, will, I truft, be a fufficient apology for themfelves. In the following pages they are *all* reftored; that the public AT LARGE may have the power to adjudge me, as well as that fmall part of it, confined within the walls of a Theatre.

Thefe paffages have not been reftored from any pertinacious opinion of their beauty— for other expreffions might have conveyed my intention as well; but had I allowed one line to ftand as altered for the ftage, what might not that reprobated line have been fuppofed to exprefs? I fhrink from the idea! And therefore moft folemnly aver, that the Comedy, as now printed, contains EVERY WORD which was oppofed the firft night, from the fufpicion of indelicacy; hoping their *obvious* meaning only will be attended to, without the coarfe ingenuity of ftrained explanations; which

have

have been made, by persons who seem desirous to surround my talk of dramatic writing, with as many difficulties as possible.

A celebrated Critic, more attended· to for the discrimination and learning which appear in his strictures, than for their *lenity*; in his observations on the Greybeards, has the following.

" When Mrs. Cowley gets possession of
" the spirit and turn of a character, she
" speaks the language of *that* character better
" than *any* of her dramatic cotemporaries."

This, I confess, I hold to be very high praise ; and it is to this very praise, which my cotemporaries resolve I shall have no claim. They will allow me, indeed, to draw strong character, but it must be without speaking its language. I may give vulgar or low bred persons, but they must converse in a stile of elegance. I may design the coarsest manners, or the most disgusting folly, but its expressions must not deviate from the line of politeness.

politenefs. Surely it would be as juft to exact from the Artifts who are painting the Gallery of Shakefpeare, that they fhould compleat their defigns without the ufe of light and fhade.

It cannot be the *Poet*'s mind, which the public defire to trace, in dramatic reprefentation; but the mind of the *characters*, and the truth of their colouring. Yet in my cafe it feems refolved that the point to be confidered, is not whether that *dotard*, or that *pretender*, or that *coquet*, would fo have given their feelings, but whether Mrs. *Cowley* ought fo to have expreffed herfelf.

This is a criterion which happily no author is fubjected to, but thofe of the drama. The Novelift may ufe the boldeft tints ;— feizing Nature for her guide, fhe may dart through every rank of fociety, drag forth not only the accomplifhed, but the ignorant, the coarfe, and the vulgar-rich ; difplay them in their ftrongeft colours, and fnatch immortality both for them, and for herfelf! I, on

the

the contrary, feel encompaſſed with chains when I write, which check me in my hap-pieſt flights, and force me continually to re-flect, not, whether *this is juſt ?* but, whether *this is ſafe ?*

Theſe are vain regrets, which I hope my readers will pardon me, for having a moment indulged. I now haſten to that part of the Comedy which will be found in the following ſheets, as *altered* for the ſecond repreſentation.

The idea of the buſineſs which concerns Antonia, Henry, and Gaſper was preſented to me in an obſolete Comedy; the work of a poet of the drama, once highly celebrated. I ſay the *idea,* for when it is known that in the original the ſcene lay amongſt traders in the city of London—and thoſe traders of the loweſt and moſt deteſtable manners, it will be conceived at once, that in removing it to Portugal, and fixing the characters amongſt the nobility, it was hardly poſſible to carry with me *more* than the idea. The circum-ſtance which moſt particularly intereſted me,

and

and fixed itſelf in my mind, was that of ſnatching a young woman from a hateful marriage, the moment before that marrige became valid—that is to ſay, after the cere-mony. This very circumſtance to which the Comedy owes its exiſtence, was that, which ſome of the audience found diſcordant to their feelings. An event which had in the laſt century been ſtampt with the higheſt applauſe, (tho' ſurrounded by many repulſive circumſtances) was found in this, to be ill-conceived. I did not, however, diſpute the deciſion of my Critics,—and the marriage has been in courſe diſſolved.

The manner in which the Comedy has ſince been received, gives room to ſuppoſe that the alteration is approved. It has ſtruggled with many oppreſſive circumſtances : the chaſm in the performance, occaſioned by the repeated illneſs of Mr. Parſons, was ſufficient to have ſunk it ;—but neither that, nor the ſterile month of December, always *againſt* the Theatres, has prevented its being dif-tinguiſhed by many brilliant and crouded nights.

nights. I now refign it to the clofet, where without the aid of fine acting, or the fafcinations of beauty, and deriving all its little force from the pen which compofed it, it hopes ftill to amufe ;—the innocent flame of Seraphina's coquetry may ftill fhed rays of delight on her readers, and the affecting fituation of Antonia intereft them.

H. COWLEY.

PRO-

P R O L O G U E.,

By Mr. COBB.

SPOKEN BY MR. BANNISTER, JUN.

PROLOGUES, like mirrors, which opticians place
In their shop windows, to reflect each face
That passes by—still mark how fashion varies ;
Reflecting Ton in all her wild vagaries :
Point out when hats and caps are large or small,
And register when collars rise or fall.
Caricature the fashionable hobby ;
And tell if boots or shoe-strings grace the lobby :
Nay, bolder grown, have fought for your applause,
With many a naughty joke on cork and gauze.
Yet howsoe'er the saucy comic muse
Delights fantastic fashion to abuse,
From pert Thalia's wit let's try to save her,
And see what can be said in fashion's favour.
How many own immortal Handel's sway,
Since fashion to the Abbey led the way !
There taking long neglected nature's part,
She hail'd him Shakespeare of th' harmonic art.
In vain had warbled Galatea's woe,
If fashion had not bid the tear to flow.
" Hailstones and fire " had spent their rage in vain ;
You might as well have heard a shower of rain.
But now, awaken'd to his magic song,
Folks wonder how the deuce they've slept so long.

3.   His

His tortur'd airs, all voices made to fuit,
His choruffes adapted for a flute.
Hand organ, hurdygurdy, tambourine ;
In Handel's praife all join the general din.
When Mifs is teiz'd to fing by every gueft ;
And fond Mamma, too, joining with the reft,
Cries, " Get the new guittar Papa has bought you ;
Play the laft leffon Mr. Tweedle taught you."
Mifs hems and fimpers—feigns a cold of courfe ;
After the ufual " Dear Sir, I'm fo hoarfe,"
Inftead of a cotillon from her book,
Where favour'd Handel triumphs o'er Malbrouk.
By way of prelude to the charming fquall,
Thrums like a minuet the March in Saul.
Papa too, who a connoiffeur now grows,
Accompanies divinely—with his nofe.
Since mufic is fo univerfal grown,
Shall not our Mourning Bride its influence own ?
Sure 'tis the wifh of ev'ry female breaft
That harmony may foothe her cares to reft.
Guided by *harmony's* enchanting laws,
Her fweeteft mufic will be your applaufe.

D R A.

DRAMATIS PERSONÆ.

Don Alexis, - - -	Mr. KING.
Don Gafper, - - -	Mr. PARSONS.
Don Octavio - - -	Mr. PALMER.
Don Henry, - - -	Mr. KEMBLE.
Don Sebaftian, - -	Mr. BANNISTER, Jun.
Donna Seraphina, -	Mifs FARREN.
Donna Antonia, - -	Mrs. CROUCH.
Donna Viola, - -	Mrs. BRERETON.
Donna Clara, - -	Mrs. CUYLER.
Rachel, - - - -	Mrs. WRIGHTEN.
Cartola, - - - -	Mrs. WILSON.

Bride Maids, Ladies, Servants, &c.

SCENE, Portugal.

SCHOOL for GREYBEARDS;

OR, THE

MOURNING BRIDE.

ACT I.

SCENE, *An Apartment at* Don Sebaſtian's.

Enter two Servants, on oppoſite ſides.

Pedrillo.

SO our Maſter is dreſſing, to dine with Don Gaſper to-day, previous to the wedding ceremony.

Jaquez. Yes—Gad the bride will be well
match'd! there's hardly a richer man in Liſbon.

Pedrillo. Well married you mean;—as to the
match, you might have made a better, between a
canary bird and a jack-a-lantern. Sixty-five and
eighteen, is a union full as vapoury and unna-
tural.

B   *Jaquez.*

Jaquez. Now you have done it! Prithee who can that ftranger be, fo muffled up, without?

Pedrillo. I know not—he takes as much pains to hide his face, as tho' he had ftol'n it.

Jaquez. Silly!—ftol'n faces are always fhewn off the moft boldly; witnefs our Ladies, after they have been robbing the rouge pots. But as to this ftranger! he fays he comes from our Mafter's friend, Don Henry.

Pedrillo. Hah! does he fo? What that Don Henry who was obliged to fly, for having fought a duel?

Jaquez. The fame. Hang me if I'd be playing at hide-and-feek in foreign lands, for drawing a little blood. I'd go boldly to court, and afk to fpeak to the Queen's Majefty, and fall upon my knees, and fay——

Pedrillo. Hift; here comes Don Sebaftian.

(*Enter* Sebaftian.)

Here is a ftranger waiting without Sir.

Sebaf. Who is he?

Pedrillo. Truly, Sir, I can't difcover. I have queftion'd and crofs queftion'd him to no purpofe ——he's as dexterous at fhifting an anfwer, as tho' he was fofter-brother to a lawyer.

Jaquez. But he fays, Sir, he came from Don. Henry,—he who was oblig'd to fly his country for challenging the ——

Sebaf. Hah! Where is he? (*going to the wing*) No, bring him hither—bring him inftantly! The brave unfortunate Don Henry! This hour will be to him, the heavieft of his life. (*he enters*) Welcome, Sir! the friend of Don Henry cannot find a houfe in Portugal, where he would be more joyfully received.

3 .   *Henry.*

Henry. What, Sir! dare you thus receive the friend of a banifh'd man?—of a man, who were he feen in Lifbon, would have his head claimed the next hour, by the executioner? If thus you can receive his friend, how will you receive himfelf? (*Throwing open his cloak.*)

Sebaf. In my arms, and in my heart! I re——no, I do not rejoice. Oh Don Henry, what imprudence! How dare you venture hither before your pardon has been obtained?

Henry. Could you fuppofe the intelligence of Antonia's marriage, would fuffer me to reft in any other fpot, that the proud fun vifits? Had I been beneath the zone from whence he pours his broadeft rays, or in the dufky regions of Cimmeria, fuch intelligence muft have impell'd me hither!

Sebaf. And to what purpofe? Surely this is a fort of Quixotifm, that muft end, like the fublime Knight's contention with the windmills.

Henry. I care not how it ends. The difpleafure of my fovereign, and my heart torn by the ingratitude of the woman on whom it doats—the fooner the end approaches, the better!

Sebaf. I am not now to learn, how hard it is, to ftem the torrent of your paffions—yet if you would be patient, all might be well.—At leaft I truft fo; tho' my vifit to England, at that period, prevented my knowing precifely the ground of your quarrel.

Henry. Quarrel! (*with contempt*) Do you then fufpect it was *a fray* in which I fought; or that my fword is drawn in tavern brawls; or to fupport the infolence, or perfidy of an abandoned wanton? Duels of that fort, a foldier ftoops not to!

Sebaf. Pray then inform——

Henry.

Henry. I fought to punifh the flanderer of him, who taught me *how* to fight—the brave D'Almeida; that once conquering hero!

Sebaf. I knew him well.

Henry. 'Twas he firft plac'd a fword upon my youthful thigh; and drawing forth the burnifh'd blade, never my Henry, faid the hoary general —— " never be its luftre ftain'd, except to ferve your king, or vindicate your friend! Thefe are the outlines of a foldier's duty;—would you be a perfect foldier? Labour to be an exemplary man!" with *that* fword——I thank it! (*holding his fword, and bending over it*) I punifh'd *his* traducer!

Sebaf. Surely you cannot doubt of pardon.

Henry. But, whilft I wait for pardon in another kingdom, my Antonia's loft—oh!

Sebaf. Is fhe not already loft?

Henry. No, fhe is not—and by heaven fhe fhall not! She's my contracted wife;—no power on earth can make her another's, whilft I live.

Sebaf. All this, my friend, only proves the bitter excefs of your difappointment—have you any fettled fcheme?

Henry. I have.—At Madrid it chanc'd that Don Julio, nephew to old Gafper my rival, conceived a warm attachment for me.—From him I learnt the news of this abhorr'd marriage— the agonies it threw me in, he compaffionated; and formed a fcheme, which wears a face of fuccefs.

Sebaf. Alas!—it is—well, but pray go on.

Henry. Learning that my perfon was unknown to Don Gafper, whofe retired life throws him out of all public circles, Julio conceived the refolution to make me pafs for himfelf.

Sebaf.

Sebaſ. You to paſs for Don Gaſper's nephew—well!

Henry. With this view he pretended an ardent deſire to viſit Portugal. His father has in courſe written to Don Gaſper; we both arrived laſt night, and Julio has given me the letter, which will fix me in the houſe of my rival; to prevent, by whatever means that may offer themſelves, the deſign upon my honour—the robbery of my wife!

Sebaſ. My dear unhappy Henry, ſummon your fortitude whilſt I tell you, that Don Julio's friendſhip, united with your own temerity, cannot ſave your honour—if your honour is to be wounded by—(*ſhaking his head.*)

Henry. What's that? oh ſpeak Sebaſtian—my apprehenſions choak me!

Sebaſ. I cannot give ſound to words ſo cruel—but fly, and ſave that life, which if you are diſcovered here, muſt be forfeited.

Henry. Hah—I underſtand you—ſhe's married! ſhe's married! Antonia is another's! Oh, Sebaſtian — let me breathe! (*throwing himſelf on Sebaſtian.*)

Sebaſ. Courage man! if you would but ſwear a little now, and give all the ſex, black, brown, and yellow, to the devil, I ſhould have ſome hopes of you.

Henry. Oh!

Sebaſ. There's no bearing this! a fine young fellow yielding himſelf to deſpair, at the very moment his perfidious miſtreſs is giving herſelf to another! This very day ſhe weds Don Gaſper.

Henry. This very day ſaid'ſt thou?—oh, ſpeak it again Sebaſtian—bleſs me with the ſound! is it this very day?

Sebaſ. Alas! he's mad.

Henry.

Henry. Oh, no; if it be *but* this day, there yet are hopes.——

Sebaf. She is now in the house of your rival. According to the custom of our country, she this morning went there, attended by her bride-maids; and in the evening old Gasper receives her vows.

Henry. They are mine!—in the face of heaven, and before witnesses they are mine;—if she has given them to another they cannot be valid, but by my assent. I'll fly instantly to the house—

(going.)

Sebaf. Nay, suffer me to attend you; for tho' I have dear and tender cares of my own, I shall scarcely be awake to them, whilst my friend is in such danger!

Don Henry. Oh, Sebastian! the bliss or misery of all my years to come, must be determined before the approaching night hath told out half its hours. The enterprize is difficult — is full of danger! but what danger can be formidable to a wretch, who, precipitated on a gulph, must leap it, or be lost?   [*Exeunt.*

S C E N E *changes to* Don Gasper's.

He enters, meeting Rachel.

Don Gasper. Well Rachel, how is my little girl? how is the bride? Are her spirits got up? What does she do?—What does she say?

Rachel. Oh lord, Sir, she says but little; and as to doing, a half stifled sigh pops out now and then, or else she's as still as an ivory statute.

Don Gasp. Statute! but why don't you talk to her then, *Mrs. Statute*; and tell her how happy
she

she is? You should say d'ye see ma'am what a fine house you are mistress of?—d'ye see ma'am how many servants are at your command?—and this rich casket of jewels ma'am, which my master presents to you—how many ladies will envy you these jewels!—Did not her eyes sparkle when she found 'em on her toilet?

Rachel. No, Sir; but they glitter'd—for there was a tear in each.

Don Gasp. Tear! ay tears of joy, to be sure!

Rachel. The bride-maids and the rest of the ladies endeavour'd all they could to divert her, but to no purpose—so I up, and said—says I, laws! ma'am, you are the happiest lady in Portugal. My master is the most agreeablest man for an old—I mean a middle-aged gentleman—that was the word indeed, Sir! for a middle-aged gentleman in all the world. He's never out of temper, nor peevish, except when he has got the gout.

Don Gasp. Pshaw!

Rachel. Then says I, Ma'am, as to wrinkles—Lord, what signifies minding a few wrinkles? Why, in forty years, Ma'am, you'll be as wrinkley as he is.

Don Gasp. What the devil did you talk to her of wrinkles for? Wrinkles! to be sure I have the crow's feet about my eyes; but many men have them before they are thirty.

Rachel. That's true. Then says I, as to my Master's teeth, Ma'am, they are as white, and even, and polish'd—ay, as your Ladyship's! And so they are you know, Sir—they have been home but a fortnight.

Don Gasp. Zounds! Get into the kitchen, and go near your Lady no more. Was there ever such a stupid chattering——

Rachel.

Rachel. It's nuts to me to fting him, for I pity the poor young creature from my foul.   [*Exit.*

Don. Gafp. I don't know whether it is ftupidity or archnefs in the wench—I am afraid fhe means to laugh at me.   Hang me if I would have married at all, if my fon would have married; but families muft be kept up; and nothing can perfuade that young dog into the trammels—he'd rather turn monk than turn to matrimony. (*Enter fervant*) Well, you faw your Lady, honeft Peter?

Peter. Yes, Sir.

Don Gafp. Ah—well—well—isn't fhe a pretty tight thing? Look in the garden—there fhe trips —there fhe trips.

Peter. With fubmiffion, Sir, I wifh the *trip* may'nt have been your's.   I am afraid this marriage is one of the falfeft fteps your worfhip ever made.—And here's my young mafter—I am out, if he does not think fo too, for all he looks fo full of fpirits.

Don Gafp. What care I for what your young mafter thinks, or you either, you old——
                              [*Exit fervant.*

(*Enter* Octavio.)

Octavio. Joy to you, Sir! joy on this feftive morn! but by the way it is very ill drefs'd for a bridal morn—the fame dufky blue it has worn this fortnight; nor has the fun been at the expence of one ray extraordinary! All nature fhould have been in gala, on fuch an event as your nuptials. —But where is my mother? I came eagerly to pay my duty.

Don Gafp. Mother! Gad it will look odd, to fee fuch a ftrapper as you, call her mother.
                              Octavio.

Octavio. Shall it be mamma, Sir?

Don Gasp. No. *Madam*—that's grave and comely. Madam has a diftant found in it—you fhall call her madam. But inftead of coming dutifully to congratulate me Sir, why did you not dutifully marry yourfelf?

Octavio. Faith, Sir, of all the duties fate has impofed upon a man, I think that the hardeft.

Don Gasp. 'Tis an impofition that fome hundred dozen of your great-grandfires, as wife and as witty as your worfhip, have fubmitted to.

Octavio. 'Tis devilifh ftrange, that it was neceffary for fo many great men to play the fool, to bring me into exiftence!

Don Gasp. There's Don Alexis d'Alva has been half mad to give you his daughter—ever fince your return from Italy.

Octavio. Ay; had I had the grace to humour him, Sir, how happy for your fair Antonia! She might have become at the fame moment a virgin bride, and a grandmamma. *(Drawling.)*

Don Gasp. Pfhaw—nonfenfe!

Octavio. However, Sir, let her not defpair—fhe may hope for the honour of being a *grand*-mother yet. I refufed the daughter of Don Alexis, without having feen her; but now that I have feen her, I think I could venture to exchange my dear prized liberty, for captivity with her.

Don. Gasp. Say you fo my boy? Its the happieft news that I have heard. But where could you fee her? for Don Alexis is fo nicely jealous, that if his ftone walls had eyes, he'd never fuffer either his wife or daughter to unveil before them.

Octavio. I faw her at church with her father. The fermon was on Chriftian charity, and to fhew

C   how

how well fhe could illuftrate the doctrine, fhe lifted
her veil on that fide next me—for fhe faw me
hungering, and thirfting, for a view.

Don Gafp. Memorandum—My wife never goes
to church.

Octavio. You fhock me, Sir——What is my
dear mamma to turn heathen?

Don Gafp. No, Sir—I'll read homilies to her,
and fhe fhall have prayers at home.

Enter Servant.

Serv. Don Alexis de Alva, Sir, is come to pay
his compliments to you on your wedding.

Octavio. 'Tis a happy prefage!—Pray recommend my fuit Sir, and in the mean time I'll go
and afk bleffing of the young lady in the garden.

[*Exit.*

Enter Don Alexis.

Don Alexis. So my old friend, you're going to do
a wife deed to day; Soloman and the child was
nothing to it! Give ye joy—I give ye joy!

Don Gafp. You have a happy knack in your ci-
vilities. You wifh me joy, as tho' you hoped it
would be forrow; and congratulate with an air of
reproach.

Don Alexis. Air of a fiddle-ftick's end! Why
didn't ye afk my advice? Could any body have
given ye better? Have I not done the fame thing
—have I not made an old afs of myfelf, by marrying a girl?

Don Gafp. Never mind that, if your girl does
not transform your afs-fhip's ears to horns.

Don Alexis. Ay, that's a bleffed fear to be
goaded with, in the laft ftage of one's mortal jour-
ney!

ney! I wiſh the day I left my bed to marry, I had been confined in it with a gout, an aſthma, and a dropſy. Oons man, there's no end of your plagues from this moment!

Don Gaſp. Pray keep your temper now—keep your temper. 'Tis a very bad one ; but pray keep it however !

Don. Alexis. Why, you'd find it eaſier to ſpin cables out of cobwebs; or to pierce thro' the earth, and ſwim out at the Antipodes, than to manage a young rantipole wife, and ſo your ſervant—I give ye joy—much good may it do you.

                             [going.

Don Gaſp. Stay, ſtay, a moment, man! and tell me which is the greateſt torment, a young wife, or daughter ?

Don Alexis. Oh lord! why a daughter is a ſeventh day ague, and a wife is a frenzy fever.

Don Gaſp. Well, come, I'll recommend ye a phyſician for your ague,

Don Alexis. A phyſician—What d'ye mean ?

Don Gaſp. Why a lover to take your daughter off your hands.

Don Alexis. Who'll be the bold man to do that?

Don Gaſp. An impudent young raſcal ſix feet and a half high; who upon ſuch authority as huſbands are obliged to take, calls me father; if you like it, he may call _you_ ſo.

Don Alexis. What Octavio! Will he be my doctor!—Octavio marry my daughter!—But perhaps this is a wedding day joke of yours, old Signor! Gad you'll find this day's work no joke believe me.

Don Gaſp. If its a joke you have it but at ſecond hand; the original inventor is now in the

houfe, and has juft defired me to employ all my
intereft in his favour.

Don Alexis. Intereft—let him ufe his own intereft—bid him come. Oh the ftout rogue!—
Your intereft! you have no more than a corkcutter
with an archbifhop. Bid him come, I fay! I'll
hurry home and prepare my daughter. Ay,
ay, let boys and girls marry, my old friend, but
as for—well I'll fay no more—much good may it
do ye!   [*Exit.*

Don Gafp. By Saint Jeffery the old fellow has
made me feel chilly upon the bufinefs!—What
brought him here to throw cold water upon all my
ardors, and all the pretty little loves that were
fpringing up, and warming the Lapland region
about my heart. In one's wintry age thofe gleams
require to be cherifh'd, and not—Gad I'll go to
little Tony—the baggage has never yet given me
one kifs; the warm touch of her lips will be an
antidote to his cold poifon, or I'm—(*going.*)

Enter Servants.

Serv. Sir, here's one Don Julio from Spain.
Don Gafp. Hey!
Serv. Your worfhip's nephew, Sir, from Madrid.   He has brought you a letter from his father,
Don Henriques; and defires you'll admit him to
pay his duty.
Don Gafp. Hah! my own fifter's fon—my poor
Olivia's boy, of whom fhe died in childbed. Let
him come in. (*Don Henry introduced.*) My dear
nephew, why I am as glad to fee thee as if—how
doft do? Grown up a man! dear, dear, how time
flips! 'Twas but yefterday that your mother came
out of the Convent to be married.——Like her
                                                too

too—very like her indeed! Well, and how doſt do Julio? how is thy father?

Don Henry. Don Henriques was well, Sir, when I left Madrid—that letter will inform you of his wiſhes. Scarcely can I contain my feelings! I am now under the roof with the perfidious Antonia—and this wretch will call her his *wife!* Let him be-ware how he ſhews the ſlighteſt fondneſs! by heaven if he ſhould——

Don Gaſp. Ay, very well—very well. Your father deſires you may be receiv'd as my gueſt; and adds, that you are of a remarkable ſober ſeri-ous turn. I am glad of it Julio—never be wild my boy! I ſuppoſe you can ſee a pretty woman without wiſhing her huſband at the devil; or en-deavouring to perſuade her, that you are a finer fellow than he is.

Don Henry. Thoſe are not my habits, Sir.

Don Gaſp. I believe ye—there's ſomething in your look that confirms what you ſay. Well you are come in happy time—you are going to have a new aunt—I'll preſent ye to her. But ſhe is very rigid;——Remember that! ſhe'll expect ye to treat her with the moſt *diſtant* reſpect. She's not ſo young as ſhe looks; no—no—a ſedate perſon. Some women will look young in ſpite of years.

Don Henry. True, Sir; as ſome men will be fools in ſpite of wrinkles.

Don Gaſp. Ay, you are right nephew—'tis a vile fooliſh age!—Now I'll carry ye to your aunt—hah, here ſhe comes;—but not ſo pretty a wo-man I aſſure you, when examined; as at the firſt glance—ſome women ſtrike at firſt, you know—

Don Henry. (*Aſide*) Hypocritical ſlanderer! How ſhall I contain my emotions? (*Antonia enters with*

with ladies) Hah! fhe doth not look happy—fome confolation to my rack'd heart!

Don Gafp. Come deary, cheer up, cheer up! What all thefe trinkets, and rich laces, and finery, not brighten ye? Had you married a young fellow, he'd have made you no fuch prefents—his money would have been lavifh'd on his miftreffes —I'll keep no miftreffes; no naughty women fhall feduce thy nown old man.

Antonia. (*Afide*) Naufeous! Oh Clara, my fate feems to open on me at this moment with a horror I never yet conceived!

Clara. 'Tis a moment too late fweet coufin! You have fubmitted to your *fate*, think now how to make your fate fubmit to *you*.

Gafp. Out, out, no whifpering till you grow old enough to turn backbiters! Now call up your fmiles (*patting Antonia's cheek*), and your pretty roguifh leers! Come ladies your fpirits, your wit! I thought every woman was happy on a wedding-day, whether 'twas her own or her neighbour's.

Lady. The bride's penfivenefs infects us, Sir. Mirth feems to be impertinent.

Antonia. Oh pardon me! Were my fpirits obedient to my wifhes, your reproach would have been undeferved; but tho' we can determine how to *act*, I find we cannot determine how to *feel*.

Don Gafp. Feel, feel! When I was a youngfter, women had no fuch word in their vocabulary. Can't you leave your feelings alone? Never mind 'em; and then like neglected guefts they'll be in no hurry to repeat their vifits. I have not regarded my feelings many years; and now they have learnt manners, and don't interrupt me.

Don Henry. (*Afide*) Not one chance look this
way!

way! and yet I can forgive the fweet averted eye, becaufe it fpeaks difguft to all around her.

Antonia. You know the caufe I have for forrow, and have allowed it; yet my penfivenefs ought not to throw a weight upon the day;—I *will* be better.

Don Gafp. Yes, yes, we fhall be as happy, and as faithful as two turtle-doves—fhan't we, Pet?

Antonia. I hope to prove my duty, Sir. He never afk'd my love! *(afide.)*

Don. Gafp. Ud! I had forgot——here, here's a nephew of mine—a nephew of *yours* now; pray receive him. Don Julio Cavallo.

(She curtfies without regarding him.)

Don Henry. *(afide)* Where then is the fecret fympathy of love, which fhould inftruct her that her Henry's near? She *fhall* obferve me.—May this day be happy to you, lady; and to him, whom moft you wifh to blefs!

(She ftarts at his voice, looks, and fhrieks.)

Don Gafp. Heyday little Pet, what ails ye?— why do you ftart and fhriek?—he's my own flefh and blood.

Antonia. Surprize, Sir. Your nephew fo much— he fo much refembles————

Don Gafp. Ay, like me, mayhap you think. I believe there is a family likenefs, but that need not have fcared you fo.

Antonia. No, Sir, it was not that——his refem- blance is to——to a moft belov'd relation, whom I have loft.

Don Gafp. Oh, what your coufin I fuppofe; that fine young man who went to Mexico, and was drown'd——ay, poor fellow he was drown'd!

Antonia. Were Don Henry living, I fhould be- lieve the ftranger him; but oh 'tis impoffible——

the

the grave will not give back its prey; no, not to
agonizing love!

Don Gaſp. Come, come, little Pudſey, what d'ye
cry for? your couſin that was drown'd, went to
Mexico to make his fortune, did'nt he?

Antonia. Yes, Sir.

Don Gaſp. Well, he got his end there—what
would you have? Come, let us go to the muſic-
room. There you, who have huſbands, will find
them; and you who have none, may make ſnares
for them. Come, Pet! *(leading her) you* are already ſnared; and egad! he muſt look ſharp who
gets you out of my net.

(*Exeunt all but Don Henry.*)

Don Henry. Yes I will look ſharp, and get her
out of thy net, cloſely as thou haſt entangled her.

(*Donna Clara returns, and twitches his arm.*)

Donna Clara. Turn, young man, I pray! (*he
ſtarts*) Good Don Julio, tell Don Henry we did
not expect to find him in maſquerade to grace Antonia's nuptials.

Don Henry. I am diſcover'd then——Oh Donna
Clara! your faithleſs couſin.

Donna Clara. Faithleſs, has ſhe been?

Don Henry. Is ſhe not this day to be married?

Donna Clara. Truly I think ſo, Signor, or I am
not a bridemaid; but how far faithleſs I know
not—for I return'd from Arragon laſt night, after
more than a year's abſence. We met but an hour
ſince in the church, nor have we yet had time for
converſation.

Don Henry. Then I entreat you let this diſ-
covery reſt with yourſelf.—It is of the laſt importance to me, that I ſhould not be known to
Don Gaſper; and at preſent, I would be equally
concealed from Antonia.

Donna

Donna Clara. You muſt give me reaſons for this requeſt; for I am ñot certain that I ought not inſtantly to betray you.   It is true, you have been her lover, but ſhe is now to be the wife of Don Gaſper;—her duties to him will be of the moſt ſacred ſort, and ſhe muſt fulfil them ſcrupulouſly.

Don Henry. Think me not a ſeducer! I have lov'd Antonia for her purity and virtue; and to deſtroy *her* honour, would be to trample on my own.   Oh Clara! few have lov'd as I do.   My paſſion is mingled with the tender protecting affection of a brother ; and violation is impoſſible!

Donna Clara. Pray then tell me———

Don Henry. You ſhall know all ;—and ſhould Antonia's marriage be voluntary, I will take no revenge but to leave her ;—but if, as her melancholy allows me to hope, ſhe has been deceiv'd into it, there's not a power on earth that can divide us.

Donna Clara. If your deſign is not contrary to rectitude, be aſſured I ſhall not oppoſe it.   Follow me to a more diſtant room——a new ſecret is almoſt as delightful as a new lover.   [*Exeunt.*

END of the FIRST ACT.

D   ACT

ACT II.

An Apartment at Don Alexis's.

Enter Seraphina, pulling in Alexis.

Seraphina.

COME along, my charming hufband! Blefs me, what eloquence and fire, confidering you are fifty nine! I próteft, a man thirty years younger could hardly have found fuch a variety of things to have faid on fo trivial a fubjeft. One might miftake you for an Englifh fenator, inftead of a Portugueze privy counfellor, you can fay fo much upon nothing.

Alex. Nothing! what is it nothing that whenever I go out of the door, your head is direftly out of the window—like the fign of Queen Jezebel? 'Tis known to all the impudent young face-hunters in Lifbon, who faunter about my gates, like wolves before a fheep-fold——d'ye call that nothing?

Seraph. Oh no ; Heaven forbid I fhould be fo ungrateful towards the grand pleafure of my life! Nothing ! 'tis *every thing*—my happinefs! I wait for funfet every day with impatience, becaufe 'tis known that I then mount my throne——that is, I enter my balcony; and fee new proftrate fubjefts adoring, and deifying me.

Alex.

Alex. Zounds! what a vile cuſtom it was to build houſes with windows! I'll have them all block'd up. Sky-lights are the only things for a Chriſtian country.——Windows and balconies!— they are fit only for Turkiſh baths, and public brothels.

Seraph. Liſten, Deary! and I'll bleſs ye with a ſecret. Blind your windows, and nail your doors, but if your honour (*curſeying*) has no better ſecurity than theſe, you'll be ſoon in the herd, whoſe ideal ornaments (*touching* his *forehead*) are ſo terrific to you.

Alex. The devil's in it if ſtone walls won't keep ye! What ſtronger ſecurity could my honour have ?

Seraph. My honour! Rely on that, and I ſwear to you by every thing ſacred, that no veſtal's life ſhall be more blameleſs. It is due to my own feelings to be chaſte—I dont' condeſcend to think of yours in the affair. The reſpect I bear myſelf, makes me neceſſarily preſerve my purity——but if I am ſuſpected, watch'd, and haunted, I know not but ſuch torment may weary me out of prin- ciples, which I have hitherto cheriſh'd as my life.

Alex. If all this is true, what the devil makes ye ſo fond of admiration ?

Seraph. I can't tell what devil makes me ſo fond of admiration ; but I know I love admiration, and I will have it ; till he, whom you repreſent, ſays no.

Alex. Whom I repreſent! who's that ?

Seraph. Mercy ! who can it be, but old, ſhrivell'd, grey-pated Time ? To *his* negative I ſhall yield— but with a very ill will, I aſſure you. If the paſſion we have for admiration is wrong, let nature look to it—'twas ſhe impreſs'd it on our hearts ;

and

and it is *her* law, that to tyrannize over the peace of man, is to woman confummation of happinefs!

Alex. And yet you every one of ye pretend to be tender-hearted, and compaffionate, and all that.

Seraph. Why to fay truth, one is a fort of a paradox. At a tale of woe, I melt like Niobe; and am agoniz'd at diftrefs, if I cannot relieve it; —yet a lover's mifery is delightful! I would not abate a man who adored me a fingle figh; and fhould have no reft at night, if I thought he was fleeping quietly.

Alex. Lord have mercy! (*muttering to himfelf.*)

Seraph. Now I hope you feel yourfelf very much honour'd, that I take you fo far into my confidence.—If you have a grain of fenfe, you'll be charm'd with it.

Alex. I don't know what the devil to make of ye. Sometimes I think one thing, and fometimes another.

Enter a Servant.

Serv. Don Octavio, Sir. (*exit*)

Alex. Better he, than Cefar! I'll wait upon him directly.——Well, I am in the way at laft, to have one plague lefs however! Don Octavio is come to offer himfelf to Viola——Pray ftep, and fend her here to receive him; for I am oblig'd to go inftantly to council. I fhall but juft fpeak to Octavio, and fend him up;—charge her to receive him well——fhe fhall be married in lefs than a week. (*exit*)

Seraph. I fhall give his daughter no fuch charge, poor girl! How can fhe receive Octavio well, with her heart devoted to Sebaftian? I wonder
what

what fort of a thing this Signor is—fome wrinkled
privy counfellor, like himfelf, I fuppofe. 'Tis
very odd now, that thofe *antients* fhould take it
into their venerable noddles, that a youthful bride
is a proper appendage to their dignity ; or to
fancy that it requires no more talents to pleafe a
pretty wife, than to govern a ftupid nation. Lord!
if my deary would but fpeak the truth now, and
warn his wife brethren——Heyday ! is *this* the
Octavio ? Handfome, I vow! young! bold! *He*
a privy counfellor ! Mercy, how could I flander
him fo ? (*Enter Octav.*) Welcome, Don Octavio!
for I am inform'd that here you *muft* have welcome. The man I faw at church, I proteft.

Octav. That cruel *muft*, checks the tranfport
your welcome gave me ! May I not hope that
without a muft, you would have given me welcome ?

Seraph. Oh yes! pray hope it ; for as I think
the feafon of *hoping*, the moft delightful in our
lives, I fhould be forry to fhorten yours.

Octav. If you mean to fhorten my hope by
difappointment, 'tis kind to protract it ; but there
is a way of ending hope, enchanting Viola ! without giving defpair.

Seraph. Viola, did he call me ?

Octav. Oh permit me to believe, that the honour
your father allows me, of telling you I adore you,
is not difpleafing to you.

Seraph. Mercy, he takes me for my hufband's
daughter——delightful !

Octav. From the moment I beheld you at vef-
pers, your image has never left me.

Seraph. I vow I won't undeceive him. I take it
very ill of my image, to follow a young man about,
and keep fuch bad company without my leave.

Octav.

Octav. Whilst your difpleafure is thus playful, I can fupport it.——Oh how charming, to find the information of your face did not deceive me.

Seraph. Why what did it promife you?

Octav. Elegance, livelinefs, franknefs, and underſtanding!

Seraph. Oh dear! how our felf-love operates on every occafion. Had I receiv'd you with frowns, and given you room to believe the commands of Don Alexis unpleafant to me, you would have thought me intolerably ſtupid, and wonder'd why nature gave intelligent eyes to an ideot.

Octav. I will not defend myfelf; to be the objeſt of your raillery is an enviable diſtinſtion—pray go on.

Seraph. Nay then I have done. An enemy who won't refiſt, is not worth combating.

Octav. If you will not combat an unrefifting enemy, I hope you will condefcend to rank him with your ſlaves.——Confent to give me your chains.

Seraph. Oh, by all means—I like to increafe my captives. There! (*making as though fhe flung fomething over his neck*) there are my chains—do you feel them?

Octav. Yes, as rofy wreaths—they delight me!

Seraph. That's not what I intend. I would have you figh under them——aye, in downright earneſt too.

Octav. It is impoffible for me to figh in earneſt, unlefs you tell me the hopes Don Alexis has given me, make *you* figh in earneſt.

Seraph. What were thofe hopes, I pray?

Octav. That I ſhould have the tranſporting joy of calling you mine.

Seraph. Indeed——I can hardly think it.

Octav.

Octav. By all the tempting witch'ries of your face, and the soft Cupids in your graceful air, 'tis true! ⋅

Seraph. So pretty an oath deserves a civil reply, and I therefore protest to you, the moment Don Alexis consents to my being yours, I'll yield you my hand without reluctance. But after this frank engagement, Don Octavio, I expect you to leave me for the present—I have a peculiar reason to request this favour. Some one will come in a moment, and spoil my roguery. (*aside*)

Octav. Your commands shall ever govern me; but when may I again presume——

Seraph. I cannot tell you exactly now—be at the gate in the evening. Adieu!—adieu!
(*Running off.*)

Octav. At the gate in the evening! How sweetly that would sound, if the little villain had not matrimony in her head. Well, if I must be a slave at some time in my life, e'en let it be now—a desperate action should be done as soon as resolved on. [*Exit.*

S C E N E, Don Alexis's *Garden.*

Sebastian *and* Viola *seated on a garden chair in the front. He throws flowers at her, then rises hastily.*

Sebas. No, I swear it Viola—I'll love thee no more. No more from this instant—I am fix'd!

Viola. (*Coming forward.*) Won't you indeed? Let me look in your face, whilst you make that wicked oath.

Sebas. I could cuff you this instant for looking so pretty. Heavens! what a horrible length of time

time is before you to do mifchief! Sixteen!—The
fire of thofe eyes can't be quench'd, nor that ala-
bafter fkin fhrivell'd, in lefs than twenty years—
oh, 'tis dreadful!

Viola. You are miftaken.   The fmall pox may
fret it, the jaundice may tarnifh it—you've many
chances to behold the frightful yet.

Sebaf. Would to heaven fome of them would
arrive! You to continue fo lovely, and your father
fo cruel!

Viola. But fuppofe the change fhould happen
to my father, and he fhould favour our wifhes;—
will you then allow me to keep my charms?

Sebaf. Ay, then indeed—oh, how I would doat
on them! Not one but fhould have its feparate
fhare of paffion divided and fubdivided.—I'd
give to each a twelvemonth, and then begin
again.

Viola. Inventive love! ever the fame, and yet
for ever new!

Enter Carlota.

Carl. Blefs me, madam, Don Alexis is return-
ed;—the council is put off—he is afking for you,
and will be in the garden dire&ly.

Sebaf. 'Tis impoffible! fcarcely have I had
time to vent half the *malice* of my tendernefs—I
have been here but three minutes.

Carl. Three minutes! Oh dear—how every
woman the noon fide of twenty would rejoice,
if time meafured out his minutes as love does!
You have been here one hour and a quarter, by
the great dial at the end of the walk.

Viola. Be it hours, or minutes, you muft leave
me my Sebaftian—Should my father furprize us, I
could

could expect nothing lefs than fix months imprifonment in a garret; with the lives of the faints
for my ftudy, and bread and water for my ban-
quet.

Sebaf. Oh, I would *embrace* the punifhment, if
at the end of the period, he would allow *you* to
give me a new imprifonment.

Carl. Now you might as well have put off thofe
two fpeeches and a half to the next opportunity
—fee the confequence! here comes the old gentleman. Well, I'll not be in the mefs I affure ye
—take it all to yourfelves—(*going.*)

Viola. Oh ftay—ftay, my dear Carlota! he can't
difcern at this diftance who we are—let me run
away—I'll go into the houfe thro' the clofe walk,
and Sebaftian fhall ftay and pafs for your lover;—
it muft be fo—the danger will be lefs to you than
me.—— [*Exit.*

Carl. Upon my word—fo *I* muft be the fcape-
goat! But I won't be blamed I vow—I'll pretend
I don't know you.—'Tis very extraordinary, Sir,
(*raifing her voice*) that the gard'ner could not leave
the wicket open, whilft he threw out his rubbifh,
but you muft throw yourfelf in for more rubbifh.
—If you don't go this minute, I'll call him to bring
his bafket, and fling you out again with the reft.

Sebaf. I deteft the fubterfuge, but I muft fubmit to it.—Oh Carlota, I feel that Viola muft be
mine!—— [*Exit.*

Carl. She feels it too.—Ay, pray get you gone,
and don't miftake your neighbour's gardens again.
—There—there,—that's your way. (*Going with
him thro' the wing.*)

Enter

Enter Alexis.

Alexis. Oh you traitrefs—artful flut! this muft
be all a feint.   I clearly heard *fhe feels it too!*
that *fhe* muft concern my wife, or my daughter—
oh my blood burns!—" She feels it too!"

Carl. (*re-entering*) I wonder people are not
afhamed of themfelves, I fwear, to pretend—Oh,
dear Sir, are you here?

Alex. Am I here—cunning gentlewoman! who
was that fpark, hey? Speak thou powder-puff—
thou fnip of gauze—thou black pin! Who was
he?—Tell me truth, for I have a touchftone to
try thee by, that thou canft not evade.

Carl. I never thought of afking who he was.
The carelefs gard'ner left the door open—he's
fome curious ftranger walking about the ftreets
of Lifbon.

Alex. Ay; feeking whom he may devour.   But
come—what were the curious ftranger and you
talking about—What were his parting words?

Carl. (*Afide.*) The devil is furely prompting
him! Why, Sir, they are not worth repeating,
he was faying 'twas——he afked if it was paft
twelve o'clock.

Alexis. (*Afide*) Is it paft twelve? (*going a little
off*) " She feels it too!" that fits like cuftard and
cucumber.   Thofe were not the words miftrefs—
try again! I mean his expreffion juft before you
faid, pray get ye gone.

Carl. Oh that, Sir—then he faid—what he faid
juft then was—that's a fine poplar! (*pointing
to a tree.*)

Alexis. (*Afide*) " A fine poplar," " fhe feels it
too." That does not meet a bit clofer than
t'other.

t'other. Come, once more comb-brufh, recollect! or by St. Anthony——

Carl. Now I have it, Sir; I have recollected now the very words—what the gentleman faid at going away, was——oh, you little black-ey'd rogue!

Alexis. (*Afide*) " You little black-ey'd rogue"— " fhe feels it too!" As wide as Lifbon harbour, from the Irifh channel. Now by our lady, if thou doft perfift in giving me the trouble to queftion thee again, this cane and you fhall be better acquainted than your fkin and your bones, huffey! (*fhaking her.*)

Carl. Oh how you gripe my arm! devil take it, if you will have it, hear it then! He faid, " I feel that Viola muft be mine." (*Bawling.*) Now are you fatisfied?

Alexis. " I feel that Viola muft be mine"— " fhe feels it too!" H—h—b—m!—that fits like the two fhells of an oyfter. (*Afide.*) Now minx, I feel that I have the truth; and I feel a violent defire to make you feel this cane. And fo that curious ftranger muft have been Don Sebaftian, whom I have order'd her never to think of— never—never!—

Carl. Why, Sir, fhe has ordered herfelf never to think of him; but lord, her thoughts mind *her* no more than a conclave of Cardinals would you— they will gallop towards him in fpite of her.—

Alexis. Will they? but I'll cripple their fpeed— they fhall have a check rein before fhe's aware. I'll go this moment, and—oh here madam comes!

Enter Viola.

Viola. Blefs me Carlota,. where have you been?

Alex. Oh dear, why fhe has been fo kind to
E 2   entertain

entertain one of your lovers without doors, madam, whilst you were engaged with another within.

Viola. I do not understand you, Sir.

Alex. You don't! Come troop mistress (*to Carlota*) you little black-ey'd rogue!

Viola. To be sure my father's bewitch'd. (*Aside.*)

Alexis. I'll fit ye! you shall pack up your wardrobe in your pocket handkerchief you little black ey'd rogue! and beat your march before you are three hours nearer your wrinkles.———

Carl. I hope I shall never overtake my wrinkles if they are to make me so suspicious and tyrannical, as your's have made you.   [*Exit.*

Alexis. Well innocent ones, what sort of entertainment did you give Octavio?

Viola. Sir!

Alexis. How did you like him?

Viola. Bless me, what has he got in his head? (*Aside.*)

Alexis. Did you coquet, and give yourself only the *allow'd* airs on these occasions; or was your stubborn mind so full of Sebastian, that you gave him no hopes?

Viola. My dear father, if you'll be pleas'd to speak in a way that I can understand——

Alexis. Don't provoke me! What encouragement, I say, have you given Don Octavio? have you dar'd to throw cold water on his hopes? Why how you stand—if you don't answer me——

Enter Seraphina, hastily.

Seraph. Bless me, my dear, what is all this noise?

Alexis.

Alexis. Why I can't get her to fay a word about
Octavio;—I know no more than my fhoe-ftring
whether fhe behav'd decently to him or not.

Seraph. To be fure fhe did—how can you
queftion it? But you are really very coarfe; allow fomething to her delicacy!

Viola. I believe they are both befide themfelves. (*Afide.*)

Seraph. Leave her with me—I'll get out all
that paft—fhe'll be undifguis'd to me.

Alexis. Gad I'll go to Octavio himfelf – that's
the fhorteft way. I'll afk *him* what paft—if he is
content, I fhall be fo. I'll go to Octavio! [*Exit.*

Seraph. Ha, ha, ha, my dear Viola, this is a
web of my weaving—how I fhall puzzle thro' it,
I know not. And your poor father—ha, ha, ha,
how you ftare! be pleas'd to know then that I have
juft been receiving the moft violent love in the
name of your ladyfhip——actually perfonating
you!

Viola. Perfonating me?

Seraph. Your father went out this morning,
my dear, and either begg'd, borrow'd, or ftole a
lover for ye.—The poor youth was introduced to
my apartment—took it for granted that I was
Viola; and begun (as I fuppofe he promis'd your
father he would) to adore, and die for me, in
very good form.

Viola. Oh, now the myftery is clear'd—this is
the Don Octavio——

Seraph. Yes, yes—now you have the nut—fhall
we crack it, or throw it away?

Viola. Pray let us get at the kernel. If you
can contrive to keep my father in the dark fome
little time, it will allow me to concert meafures
with

with Don Sebaſtian. You do him the honour to approve his addreſſes, I know.

Seraph. Oh, if you can make any thing of the incident, it is quite at your ſervice. I'll liſten to Octavio's love-tales with all the condeſcenſion imaginable; and let him adore me, for a month to come, if it will be of uſe to you and Sebaſtian.

Viola. How very grateful he will be!

Seraph. Well, let us go then and ſettle matters. We muſt take Carlota into our council, or the thing can't go on.

Viola. My father has diſcharged her.

Seraph. Pho, I'll manage that. It would be hard, indeed, to marry an old man, and not make him do as one likes. Young huſbands we are content to ſubmit to, but when we marry GREY-BEARDS, it is with the pious deſign to have our way in every thing. [*Exeunt.*

END of the SECOND ACT.

ACT III.

An Apartment at Don Gasper's.

Enter Don Henry, hastily, followed by Don Sebastian.

Henry.

OH 'tis too much!

Sebas. Too much! ay, so it is, that they should be all so blind to your starts, your angry blushes, and your ill conceal'd confusion. I drew you from the company the moment dinner ended, lest when they had done eating they should begin to observe. Do you reflect that Don Philip has only to betray you to the minister, to get rid of his rival for ever?

Henry. It is more than I can bear—the old dotard's fondness, which I dare not yet oppose, distracts me! Oh that I could speak to her alone! —'tis plain amidst all the bridal gaiety her heart is not at ease.

Sebas. Your wish is half answered, for here comes *her* half—the worst half indeed by forty years.

Henry. Half! thou a lover, and able to speak thus *to* a lover? Speak of them as *one!*

Sebas. Forgive me! for faith I am so much a lover at this moment, that I scarcely know what I am saying. In a word, I am summon'd by my mistress's maid, who has some new information— in an hour I am again at your service.   [*Exit.*

Enter

Enter Don Gaſper.

Don Gaſp. Why how now Julio! What ſtole a-
way?—run from the gueſts—hide in corners—
how's this?

Henry. I am not in ſpirits for company, Sir; or
to be ſure this joyful occaſion——

Don Gaſp. Not in ſpirits on your uncle's wedding-
day—out upon it!—But tell me boy what do you
think of the bride?—Am I not a happy man—
hey?

Henry. If it turns out ſo, Sir.

Don Gaſp. Oh, I fear no turns. She is virtuous
and modeſt, and you know a modeſt woman is
above all price—but perhaps you do *not* know
that; for the obſervation is made in a book not
much read now a days.—But what d'ye think
help'd me to get her?

Henry. Ay, Sir, what did?—I long to be inform'd. Wine perhaps will make him communi-
cative. (*Aſide.*)—A ſplendid jointure probably.

Don Gaſp. Jointure! ſhe minds a jointure no
more than a jointed doll—gueſs again!

Henry. I am not fortunate in gueſſing.

Don Gaſp. Then I'll tell ye—half a ſheet of
paper got her. Ay, you may well ſtare. 'Twas
but half a ſheet of paper—in which I procured it
to be ſaid, that one Don Henry, whom ſhe lov'd,
was ſhrouded and buried—that got her my boy!
(*ſlapping him on the ſhoulder*)—there's a contriving
uncle for you!

Henry. Is it poſſible?

Don Gaſp. Poſſible, why I *did* it—I did it. And
where's the harm? A baniſh'd man is a dead man

in

in the eye of the law, and a dead man can be no husband. He fought a duel and was forced to fly.

Henry. And how, Sir, could you take advantage————

Don Gasp. Why those young rascals take every advantage over us, with nature to back 'em; and we have a right to make reprisals when we can by the help of art.

Henry. And so the lady believed your intelligence?

Don Gasp. Yes, yes, she believ'd—and swoon'd —and raved—and took to her bed. Faith the doctor gave her up; but I still determined when it came to the last gasp, to tell her the truth, rather than have her death to answer for—but it never came to that.

Henry. No, no! female grief, tho' sometimes obstinate, is seldom fatal. Why, my dear uncle, you are a perfect Machiavel at a plot. I shall try if I can't out-plot you though. (*Aside.*) It will be amusing to see Antonia's astonishment, when she finds her Henry is still living—ha, ha— but then she'll be your's, ha, ha, ha.

Don Gasp. Yes, then she'll be mine—she'll be mine! ha, ha, ha, You must know the chit had no fortune, tho' of a noble family—was pester'd with youthful profligate lovers, and at length to get rid of them, agreed to give herself to me—— there's a stroke of prudence in a girl!

Henry. (*Aside.*) Oh, 'twas more;—I feel it was a stroke of love to *me!* But what will Don Henry say to this pretty jest, which you and I find so laughable?

Don Gasp. What care I what a man says a thousand miles off.

F

Don

Henry. But if he obtains his pardon, he'll return, and then————

Don Gasp. Pardon! Oh, you don't know how deep I am.—I leave no loop-holes for my schemes to drop through. Hark in your ear—but be secret —I have bought his pardon.

Henry. How, Sir——bought his pardon!

Don Gasp. Hush! that's all under the rose—— you understand me—it cost me a good lump of moidores!

Henry. You astonish me!—Strange kindness to a man whom you could rob of his wife!

Don Gasp. Kindness—tut! I got his pardon for myself, that nobody else should have it;——so that if he gets any one to ask for it, it will be answered, " the pardon has been already granted" —but for want of my appearance, he's defunct depend on't;—ay, as much out of the world, as tho' the sexton had cover'd him with green-sod.

Henry. And are you actually in possession of his pardon?

Don Gasp. As good;—the money is paid, and I shall receive it from the broad-seal office to-morrow.

Henry. What a discovery is here! (*Aside.*)

(Don Alexis *enters, pulling in* Octavio.)

Alex. Come in here; come into this room, my dear Octavio! So, here's the *young* bridegroom. Now prithee be so kind to leave the apartment to me and Octavio.

Octav. Let us not disturb my father, Sir.

Alex. Disturb—a feather! Will you leave us?

Gasp. Yes, yes, I'll leave ye—but first let me

pre-

prefent my nephew to you.   The fon of my fifter Victoria—you knew her.

Alex. Knew her—ay, as well as your nofe does its fpectacles.   So, young gentleman, what you are come to dance at your uncle's wedding ? and 'twas worth while to come poft from Madrid on purpofe ;—you won't cut capers at fo wife a wedding every day, I can tell you.

Gafp. Come, come, a truce to your fneers. Don't you think he refembles his poor dear mother ?

Alex. Not a bit.

Gafp. No ! the eyes are the very fame.

Alex. Eyes !—why, her's were blue, and his are black.

Gafp. That's nothing—they've juft the fame look with 'em.

Alex. Yes. I grant ye as to the look, his look as much like eyes as her's did.   Then fhe was round favour'd.

Gafp. What fignifies that————a long face, and a fhort face, may have the fame air.

Alex. But his hair is dark, and her's was light.

Gafp. Oons ! how you talk—Why all hair muft be light, or dark, or fome colour.   Come along, nephew————When people get old, they grow fo obftinate, there's no convincing them of any thing. Come along—come along. (*Exit with Don Henry.*)

Alex. Don't take him to your Antonia, left fhe fhould have the odd notion, that he's a fitter bridegroom for her, than you are. (*Bawling after him.*) Well, my dear boy, I am come on purpofe to afk how you manag'd to-day with my daughter.   The young flut is fo mealy-mouth'd, 1 could get nothing out of her.   Was fhe kind—did fhe fhew a proper fenfe of the favour ?

Octav.

Octav. Senfe of the favour, Sir! She permitted *me* to implore the favour of being allow'd to hope.

Alex. Well, well, that's the point I would come to—hang phrafes! Was you contented with your reception——was fhe no more than decently coy?

Octav. She was all goodnefs, Sir. Why what an old fellow's this! *(afide)*

Alex. All goodnefs——well, that's in generals. Tell me—come now tell me honeftly, did fhe let you kifs her?

Octav. Heavens! I dared not let fuch a thought exift. Had any man but her father afk'd me——

Alex. You'd have faid yes;—you would, I know you would! Boafted of the fweetnefs of her lip, and of the preffure of her white hand, but I— I muft know nothing—I am an old father.

Octav. (afide) What can be the meaning of all this? Is it his fufpicion, or his folly?

Alex. Come, why won't you tell me now?— Tell me at once.

Octav. What fhall I tell you, Sir?

Alex. What!—why that fhe treated ye kindly— that you liked her pouting lips; and that————

Octav. Believe me, Sir, I dared not attempt fuch a liberty.

Alex. No! why had you not my permiffion?

Octav. I did not fo confider it, Sir; but if you'll lay your commands on the lady, when I have the honour to wait on her again————

Alex. Ay, that I will, never fear me. But pray where's the foundation of your great content, if nothing kind paft? I fear the flut has deceiv'd him. *(afide)*

Octav. Kind! fhe was all angelic fweetnefs, Sir!

Alex.

Alex. Pho! don't tell me of *angelic* fweetnefs; a young fellow fhould be content with nothing lefs than *mortal* fweetnefs, when with a blooming girl.

Octav. She had the condefcenfion to promife—

Alex. What—what?

Octav. That when you fhould order her to beftow her hand on me, fhe would obey you without reluctance.

Alex. She promis'd *that*, did fhe?

Octav. She did; and my delighted foul hath dwelt on the found from that moment.

Alex. Well, well, come again this evening, and your foul fhall have fomething elfe befides found to dwell upon, or I'll underftand why.

Octav. Good Sir, you would be very conveni-ent I perceive, but it unfortunately happens, that I chufe the fweet trouble of getting over my love difficulties myfelf.

Alex. Oh to be fure—above being oblig'd I fee! but I tell you thefe young baggages have all their arts to make a man half mad, and I know 'em—I'll manage her my little Octy, never fear! Sound indeed!

Octav. Allow me, Sir, with all humility, to re-queft that you'll give yourfelf no trouble in the bufinefs. S'death! If I don't take care I fhan't have the pleafure of running down my own game. If you wifh to make a fon-in-law of me, Sir, you muft permit me to travel the road of love in my own manner.—No bearing him! [*Exit.*

Alex. Zounds! what a heat you're in! Why, fo you may travel the road of love in your own manner—I only mean humbly to open the turn-pike gates for ye.—See what one gets by one's good nature! (*Exit.*)

SCENE.

SCENE. Don Gafper's *Garden*.

Enter Henry.

Don Henry. (*looking, as tho' uncertain.*) Surely
'tis herfelf—yes, 'tis Antonia! Like the foft lilly
prefs'd by the dewy robe of night, fhe bends her
lovely head. Oh Clara! lead her—lead her to her
Henry! Hah—accordant to my wifh they come!
But how may I be mafter of her thoughts? Perhaps to her friend, fhe will unveil her inmoft heart.
I'll feem to fleep—yes; but whilft I appear to
flumber, my ear will hang on every found fhe ut-
ters, and my whole foul be fufpended on her
breath. (*He reclines on a bank. Some fhrubs prevent his being immediately feen.*)

Enter Antonia *and* Clara.

Cla. This is the ftrangeft whim! feeking fhades
and folitude, inftead of company and mirth.
What will Don Gafper fay?
Ant. Oh name him not; the arrival of the
young ftranger his nephew, has renewed all my
miferies. But here my forrows have a fhort cef-
fation. Oh, how thofe lonely fhades will footh
my fadnefs! Each day I'll feek the foft recefs, and
opening all the treafures of remembrance, live on
my Henry's image.
Clara. Come, come, that's a fort of image worfhip we don't allow. It would be more catholic
to live in lonely fhades with himfelf. "*This foft
recefs*" would be at leaft more *poetical* my dear,
with a handfome young man in it, even tho' he
fhould be uncivilly afleep. (*pointing to Henry.*)

1

Ant.

Ant. (*Not regarding her.*) Oh, I'll call˙back each facred hour which bleft our wedded˙ fouls; trace each fond fcene that chaften'd love made. pure, and in the dear review, forget that I'm a wrètch.

Cla. Ay, do forget it pray, and look behind thofe fhrubs—there's a youth as much like Don Henry, as ever one impudent rogue was like another.

Ant. Hah! 'tis Don Julio—let us retire before he wakes. And yet—Oh Clara! I could wifh his fleep lengthen'd to eternity; and myfelf immortal, to ftand thus and gaze on him!

Clara. One might almoft fancy it Don Henry himfelf; only unhappily 'tis not the cuftom for people to leave their family manfions in the churchyard, to repofe on violets for their miftreffes to gaze on them.

Ant. The refemblance is ftronger now he fleeps. When awake, this ftranger has a fcorn—a feverity in his eye—fomething that made˙ me fear; but Henry's eye talk'd only love! Oh, I have feen a volume in a fingle glance;—one look has faid, what eloquence and learning might try to imitate in vain.

[*Sings.*]

Sweet rofy fleep! Oh do not fly,
Bind thy foft fillet on his eye,
That o'er each grace my own may rove,
And feaft my haplefs, joylefs love!
For when he lifts thofe fhading lids,
His chilling glance fuch blifs forbids ——
Then rofy fleep oh do not fly,
But bind thy fillet on his eye!

Clara.

Clara. I fay on the contrary open your eyes! Who knows but they may by this time have acquired a fofter expreffion?

Ant. Fie, Clara! let us go this inftant—you will furely wake him. (*going baftily.*) [*Exit* Clara.

Henry. (*Starting up.*) Yes, he is awakened indeed! Oh my Antonia, turn! Turn fweet traitrefs, and look upon the man you've injured!

Ant. (*Shrieking.*) Oh, I fhall fink! What art thou? Is Henry then alive in Julio? Oh tell me whilft I yet can breathe—Say, art thou both, or nothing?

Henry. Convince thyfelf. (*Embracing her.*) Oh, my Antonia!

Ant. No! 'tis not air—my arms return not empty to my bofom, but meet a folid treafure!

Henry. A treafure you have lightly priz'd.

Ant. Alas, my Henry, I believ'd thee dead! Oh let me touch thee yet again! (*taking his hand*) Thefe veins are warm with life! health blufhes on thy cheeks; and this foft preffure darts thro' my nerves, and is new life to me. Oh my Henry! it is—it is thyfelf!

Henry. Can this joy be real? You thought me dead, Antonia, and chofe in bridal pomp to celebrate my obfequies!—The Ephefian ftory will be always new.

Ant. Think not my *heart* perfidious. Had I chofe a youthful hufband, you might have term'd me fickle—but from thofe l fled—abhorr'd a fecond love, and fix'd where venerable age fecured my heart from every tender impulfe. A guardian 'twas I afk'd, and not a hufband.

Henry. Nature made women falfe, to fee how well they would excufe their crimes.

Ant.

Ant. 'Tis well you treat me thus, to check the transport of beholding thee, which else might be too much! But think, reproachful man! consider my high birth, and slender fortunes—Behold me a lonely orphan, haunted by a train of lovers—some too high in rank to make them fear to act, whate'er their wishes prompted. 'Twas to escape all these—

Henry. Oh, was it that indeed, which forced thee to this marriage?

Ant. It cannot be a marriage since my Henry lives! My vows were given to thee—the solemn contract sign'd; and heaven, by its holy priest, invoked to bless the engagement!

Henry. And in heaven 'tis recorded!

Ant. I do acknowledge it: and death alone could give Antonia *right* to make herself another's. Base artifice deceiv'd me, and virtuous art must free me from the deceiver.—But, oh; thy life's at stake! Where shall we fly?—At what blest altar solemnize our vows?

Henry. Wilt thou then follow my sad fortunes?

Ant. Yes—to the utmost boundaries of the earth!

Henry. Oh; my sick soul needed a cordial of this mighty strength to cheer it! Know then, Antonia, we need not fly—my pardon's promis'd —I have important secrets to communicate— to-morrow thou'lt be mine.

Ant. To-morrow!

Henry. Transporting hour! And wilt thou yet be Henry's? Oh bind the promise on thy knee; —invoke the sacred powers to witness it.

Ant. Thus then! (*kneeling*) and hear me, heaven!

Henry. And thus I listen to thee. (*kneeling*)

G   *Enter*

Enter Don Philip, *followed by* Alexis.

Gasp. Tony! my little Tony, where art? Hey!
(starting)

Alex. 'Sblood! what's all this?—Ah—didn't I warn ye of the bride's odd notions?—didn't I warn ye?

Henry. We are undone!

Ant. Trust to me. *(apart)* Thus then I invoke the sacred powers to witness my resolve—Never to know another love! never to hold myself bound by any vows, but those made to the lord of my affections, the contracted husband of my heart!

Phil. Her contracted husband——mark that now. *(to Alexis)*

Henry. And thus do I invoke the same gracious powers, to bless you, as you're true; and to preserve thee and *that* husband in a sweet eternity of love! *(Don Philip runs to help them up.)*

Phil. Thank ye, my dear children! There—there, what d'ye say now to my choice? Had ever man such a wife, and such a nephew?

Alex. No faith, I believe not; and may I be hanged if I believe it now, though I have seen it.

Phil. Envy—sheer envy! You see when *I* marry a girl, *I* know how to chuse one. Come along, my pigeons. *(going off with one under each arm.)* [*Exit Philip and Antonia.*

Alex. Hark ye, Don Julio—give me a minute. *(twitching him back)* Come, I know there's some jest in this. You must trust me, and egad if you will. I'll——do trust me, I know 'tis some jest.

Henry. I admire your penetration.

Alex. I love a jest to my soul, and gad if you'll trust me—here—here's a seal ring *(taking it off)* 'twas worn by my great grandfather fifteen gene-

5   rations

rations back.   I value it beyond the great ruby in
the throne at Delhi.—Egad I have a great mind
to give it ye. (*Putting it on again, and throwing
his hand behind him.*)

Henry. An idea darts upon me!—yes, by heaven
it fhall be done! this is the critical inftant of
Antonia's fate. (*Afide.*)   A ring valued by you
fo highly, Don Alexis, ought to grace no finger
but your own—I refufe to accept it; but if you'll
entruft it to me, I fwear when you next fee it you
fhall know the jeft.

Alexis. Shall I indeed?

Henry. Yes—and I'll venture to promife that
you fhall enjoy it too!

Alexis. There's my ring.   I pant for the hour
of its being reftored, as much as a girl does to
unburthen her firft love fecret.

Henry. I too pant for the hour; for if I miftake
not, I fhall mean time make fuch a ufe of your
great grandfather's feal ring, as muft make that
and every future hour blifsful to me!   [*Exit.*

Alexis. What can he mean to do with it? that
feal ring make all his future hours blifsful! May
be there's fome conceal'd witchcraft in it, and he
has had wit enough to find it out; or if rightly
turn'd it may make a man invifible, or fomething
of that fort—there have been fuch things former-
ly.—Gad I'll follow him tho'—if my ring has any
properties of that kind, how fnugly I fhall be
able to watch my wife!

End of the Third Act.

G 2   ACT

i

ACT IV.

SCENE, Seraphina's *Apartment*.

Enter Seraphina, *followed by* Octavio.

Seraphina.

IT is in vain, and fo——

Octav. Charming Viola, why are ye fo barbarous? Is it not by your own permiffion I attend you?

Seraph. Yes, I know it is; but what of that? When the fun fhone I liked you, and now by candle light I hate you—do go, I will not be teazed.

Octav. This is fo fingular!

Seraph. What, that a woman fhould change her mind fince morning? You, I fuppofe, are fo wonderfully conftant, that you change your's only with the moon.

Octav. Do not fufpect me of ficklenefs—permit me to prove my conftancy.

Seraph. Impoffible—impoffible.

Octav. How fo?

Seraph. I fee I muft tell you, to avoid altercation. Be pleafed to know then, Sir, that there is nothing on earth I deteft like this fober, quiet,

prudent

prudent method of loving. Your vows have a *father's* approbation;—you are expected;—you enter the house without difficulty;—you yawn through an hour of common-place;—the wedding-day is fixed, and we go to church to be married, in the same hum-drum stupid way, that millions of dull couples have done before us. No, no, this I can't submit to, believe me!

Octav. Ah, 'tis plain we were born for each other, we think so exactly alike! *(aside.)* These I confess are misfortunes; but how in our case are they to be avoided?

Seraph. If you are really in earnest in your love, you must contrive to make Don Alexis hate you. Let him throw a thousand difficulties in the way, and then I'll throw *myself*—into your arms!

Octav. Oh, that extatic promise! But your father is unhappily attach'd to our marriage—What the devil can I do to make him set his face against it? I fear it is impossible.

Seraph. Poor Don Octavio! then you have no hopes—for I do swear by every thing that can bind me, whilst Don Alexis approves of our nuptials, I never will be your's.

Octav. I'll bribe fellows to slander me! was ever so unhappy a dilemma? I thought his approbation till this moment a blessing; but now I would willingly make him shut his doors against *me*, and confine *you* to a grated room, with a dozen smoak-dried Duennas to guard you.

Seraph. Ay, then indeed things would go on gloriously! You would be sighing and groaning without, and I should be weeping and wailing within. Then for plots and contrivances—then for bribes and scaling ladders—then for escapes
and

and purfuits—Oh, what would I not do for a man
who fhould bring me into fuch blifsful difficulties!

Octav. I fwear you fhall be obey'd, whatever I
hazard. Who knows but an elopement may
finifh the affair fhort of marriage! *(Afide.)* (*A
buftle without—the door opens a little, and difcovers
Carlota ftruggling to keep out Alexis.)*

Alexis. I tell you, Mrs. Brazen, I will be
amongft 'em.

Carl. Blefs me, Sir, how can you be fo barbarous to difturb the young people?

Seraph. There's Don Alexis! now begin your
tafk directly—prevent his coming in; if he enters, I never will be your's.

Alexis. Let me in I fay.

Octav. Pardon me, Sir, you muft not come in.
(Going to the door.)

Alexis. Muft not come in—why you young
dog! Well, well, tell me then, is fhe kind—
hey my little Octy! is fhe kind?

Octav. Not quite fo kind as I wifh her to be.

Alexis. Oh, a jade! You flut you—you per-
verfe baggage! I will have you kind to Octavio.

Octav. Devil take him, why does he not bid her
difmifs me? then fhe'd fly to my bofom. *(Afide.)*

Alexis. Octy! Octy! *(ftruggling with Carlota)*
have you kifs'd her yet?

Octav. No! *(loud—in paffion.)*

Alex. Then you fhall—I will fee you kifs her,
by Jove!

Carl. Lord Sir! How can you be fo rum-
bufterous?

Alex. Come *in,* I will.

Seraph. *(afide)* Then go *out* I muft.   [*Exit.*

Alex. So! what's fhe off! *(burfting in.)*
Octav.

Octav. Off! yes, and now I'll be off. What woman of delicacy could bear to be thus treated? ─Or what father but you──(*going.*)

Alex. Now dear Octy do not be angry—do not be angry! You have the character of one of the civileſt, politeſt, diſcreeteſt──

Octav. The character lies, Sir—I am none of theſe. I am rude, ill-natured, unjuſt, fickle, and full of extravagance!

Alex. Hey day! Why I believe you are full of wine too.

Octav. I am every thing you ought to dread. You could not in all Liſbon have picked out ſo hopeleſs a huſband for your daughter.

Alex. Oh Lord! no—you are a very hopeful young gentleman—The character you have given of yourſelf, would ſuit ye all I doubt;—but you ſeem ſo intimate with *your* faults, that like a ſtale acquaintance, they'll ſoon diſguſt ye—therefore fickle, drunk, or mad, my daughter ſhall be your wife.

Octav. Are you ſo obſtinate Sir!

Alex. Ay—and if ſhe dares demur—

Octav. Oh I am ruin'd—if you perſiſt I am ruin'd. Dear Don Alexis pardon me! I ſee my ſcheme was ridiculous—a better ſtrikes me. In one word—ſtay, let's take care we are not heard—in one word, you and I muſt both be in a plot, againſt your lovelely capricious daughter.

Alex. How now!

Octav. Her vivacity renders a ſtupid, formal, *allow'd* courtſhip, intolerable to her. If you perſiſt in countenancing my addreſſes ſhe will hate me; but if you order her to ſee me no more, and allow me to ſteal her out of a window, or over the garden wall, she'll be the happiest bride in Portugal.

Alex. D'ye say so? Oh a perverse baggage— but I'll fit her! Won't love ye, merely because I order her to do it! that she had from her mother!———

Octav. You must conceal your knowledge of that.

Alex. Pho! d'ye imagine I don't see your whole drift now? If you was to continue talking a Lapland winter, you could not make the hint clearer. Gad she's coming, and my wife with her. So d'ye hear you Signor Don Octavio, (*speaking loud*) you are—I say you are—you shall know what you are another time; for the present that's your way, Sir, that your way out; and I'll be sworn you shall never know the way in. (*Pushing him out.*)

Enter Seraphina *and* Viola.

Seraph. Why my dear husband is so mere a gudgeon, there's no credit in deceiving him. Now remember your lesson. (*to* Viola)

Alex. So mistress—I have dispatch'd your lover.

Viola. Have you, Sir?

Alex. A young rakeshame! your not liking him proves you have your father's penetration. Notwithstanding his modest front, there's not such a desperate fellow this side the Ganges; no nor 'tother side the Black Sea.

Seraph. My sweet love, are you speaking of Don Octavio?

Alex. Yes, I am. Take care you give him no encouragement, d'ye hear girl? No whisperings from your balcony; no private correspondences;

no

no billets dropt by your officious maid, on pretence they are meant for some carotty-pated country cousin!

Viola. Dear Sir!

Alex. No pencil'd assignations on the back of your fan; or cards in lemon juice—to be call'd on detection secret orders to your perfumer, for pearl powder, and bloom of Circassia.

Seraph. How can you put such things in the girl's head, deary?

Alex. (*aside*) That her fingers may put them in practice, to be sure; but you are not up to me there, deary! (*aside.*)

Viola. But a few minutes since, you were fearful, Sir, that he was not received with sufficient favour.

Alex. That was—that—well, no matter. That was, perhaps, to try how far things had gone.

Seraph. Oh I beg your pardon! the curtain rises, and we see the sun! Now I understand your policy—how admirable! You middle-aged gentlemen are so deep, that 'tis difficult to sift ye.

Alex. Ay, and when we are sifted——

Seraph. You are found to be chaff. Poor dear Don Octavio! Send him a garland of willows, Viola.

Viola. Rather of myrtles—he's too handsome for willows.

Alex. Handsome is he, that handsome does—remember that.

Viola. Why Sir, he does handsomely. He has travell'd handsomely, has a handsome estate, has brought home a handsome character, and now wishes for a handsome wife.

Alex. Ay, but he must go further a field to catch her though. He'll find neither wives nor widgeons in my orchard.

H

Seraph.

Seraph. No, our widgeons are all within doors.

Viola. Unfortunate that I am! juſt made up my mind to diſmiſs Sebaſtian, nay abſolutely to diſlike him, and now—

Alex. And now! why now you muſt make up your mind t'other way. Perhaps in my preſent humour, of the two fools, I like Sebaſtian beſt.

Viola. But that humour muſt change, for I can never think of thoſe two young men as you do, my dear father.

Alex. Thoughts are free, daughter! Gad I could hug her. (*aſide.*)

Seraph. You ſee your father generouſly leaves your thoughts unſhackled, my dear; he only deſires to controul your actions—pray oblige him, and take Sebaſtian.

Alex. (*aſide*) Zounds! ſhe knows nothing of our plot, and gives that advice ſeriouſly.

Seraph. He is a moſt accompliſh'd young man.

Alex. Wife!

Seraph. Engaging in his manners, and reſiſtleſs in his form.

Alex. My dear, I ſay. (*ſpitefully.*)

Seraph. His eyes are expreſſive, and his tongue is eloquent.

Alex. The devil's in *your* tongue! (*aſide.*) You don't know what you are talking of.

Seraph. I do indeed—perfectly. In ſhort, Viola, he is ſo amiable, ſo captivating, and loves you with ſuch unbounded fondneſs, that if you marry any other, your miſery ought to equal your ingratitude.

Alex. Gad ſhe ſpeaks with an air of too much conviction—this muſt be managed more nicely. To your chamber, huſſey, and try to forget Octavio.

(*puſhing off Viola.*)

Seraph.

Seraph. And remember your Sebaſtian. Let him be preſent to you waking, and ſleeping; let him——

Alex. Zounds let him alone! (*driving her off on the other ſide*) you may be doing miſchief all this while. I dare not let her into my plot, leſt her per-verſeneſs, or her folly ſhould mar it. And yet, I think—no hang it I won't—I won't. The only plot that ever had a woman in it came to nothing. I'll conduct this ſolely by my own ſagacity, and have a hearty laugh at the poor fools, when all is over.

[*Exit laughing.*

SCENE, *An elegant Apartment at* Don Gaſper's, *illuminated.*

Rachel *enters firſt; followed by* Gaſper, Antonia, Clara, *and a number of Ladies.*

Rach. (*looking back*) Bleſs us! the approach of the ceremony has made my maſter half out of his ſenſes. The poor bride too ſeems half out of her's—but not with joy—if I may gueſs.

Don Gaſp. (*capering in, and ſinging.*)

Tired of dance, of ſong, and play,
Now we end our wedding-day.

Yes, yes, now for the ceremony! Come my pretty Pet, the Prieſt is waiting in the next room to make thee the happieſt girl in Portugal. In ten minutes thou wilt be the wife of Don Gaſper de Frontado! (*ſtrutting.*)

Ant. (*Aſide*) Oh heaven! where is Henry? Rachel, my ſoul ſinks within me.

Rach. Truly, mine is not very high.

Gaſp.

Gafp. Heyday! what's all this about? What! fhe muft be coax'd now I warrant—they all love coaxing. Come now, my pretty Tony, my nown little Tony. (*Taking her under his arm.*)

Ant. (*breaking from him*) Henry! Henry! Where art thou? Oh, he mocks me!

Gafp. Come, let us to the prieft, and tie the knot, which even Alexander who cut the gordion will never be able to deftroy.

Henry. (*without.*) Where is he—the bridegroom! the happy bridegroom!

Ant. Oh my heart—he is come!

Gafp. Here he is—here is the happy bridegroom. (Henry *enters*) Come, you are juft in time to witnefs the ceremony.—The prieft waits to join us in his rofy bands. Look at her! h-u-m! Oh, you fweet little———There are fmiles and blufhes for ye! Look at her!

Henry. They are like thofe of Aurora, when fhe flies before the jolly god of day!

Gafp. And I the jolly god of day purfue her.

Henry. But charming Antonia, the blifsful fate which awaits you muft be poftponed a few hours. Oh, Sir, I am fent———

Gafp. Sent—about what! from whom?—who has fent you to poftpone Antonia's blifs?

Henry. It is happy I have a token to convince you. Here, Sir,—do you know this great feal ring? the impreffion is———ftay, can you fee it? (*taking a candle*) the impreffion is a fatyr; look at his horns.

Gafp. The devil's in fuch luck! A man on the wrong fide of fifty or fo, can't marry but at every turn he has horns in his teeth. If he's invited to a tavern, the dinner is fure to be at the *horns*: They'll *wake* me with horns to-morrow morning

8   —nay,

—nay, I am even kept from the ceremony to-night, to be regaled with the fight of *horns*.

Ant. (*to* Clara.) What can be the purport of the ring? I can hardly breathe thro' terror!

Henry. Do you know them, Sir?

Gasp. Know them! Yes—they are Don Alexis's horns, not mine—it is his ring;—but what have I to do with it, any more than with the ring of Saturn, or the belt of Jupiter? If you are for rings, you shall see one presently (*taking* Antonia's *hand*) on this waxen finger, that——

Henry. You will not hear me, Sir. This is a token from Don Alexis——observe me, Sir, a *token*; by which you are required, as a counsellor of the realm, to meet Don Alexis immediately at his own house, on affairs of imminent importance.

Gasp. Meet Don Alexis! What is he mad? or are you mad? or does he think me mad? Go, prithee——I'll meet him to-morrow. (*seizing* Antonia's *hand*) My service to his night cap! (*going.*)

Henry. To-morrow! Why, all our throats may be cut by to-morrow.

Gasp. Hey! throats cut!

Hen. Why Sir, there's a plot—a plot.

Gasp. A plot!

Clara. (*to Ant.*) Now I have his design. My dear Don Gasper, at a juncture so important, every selfish consideration must be annihilated. Should our discontented citizens take arms——

Hen. Nay, for aught I know they are in arms already.

Gasp. Arms! well what can I do? Fight dog fight bear—I'll be married. (*going.*)

Rachel. (*dropping on her knee*) Oh dear Sir, there'll be nothing but rapes and murder! Oh take pity on us poor virgins, Sir, and go.

Gasp.

Gafp. Don't be a fool! (*ftriving to get free.*)

Clara. Confider, Sir, the good of the nation.

Rach. Ay, Sir, the good of the nation ;—what wouldn't a body do for the good of the nation ?

Gafp. Good of the nation !—'twould be a fhame! Go—go Julio, and vote for me ; I'll make you my proxy.

Hen. Your proxy *there*, Sir ! No, no, excufe me. But haften ;—whilft you dally, all Lifbon may be fired.

Gafp. If there's fuch danger, I am fafeft here— an't I, duck ? (*to Ant.*)

Ant. Oh Sir, if you can refift the calls of honour, do not refift me. To marry in the midft of fuch horrible apprehenfions, is impoffible—and my fears are fo great, they will deftroy me. Sweet Don Gafper, go !

Gafp. Nay then——come, my dear Nephew, let us go together ; not a ftep will I move without you.

Hen. (*afide*) Oh miferable, to be thus circum-vented. Had I not better ftay here to guard the——

Gafp. Stay *here!*—Oh you are a dutiful Nephew. No, Sir, you fhall guard me, if I ftir—but I won't ftir by all——

Ant. Fye, Don Julio! furely you will not défert your uncle. Leave him in the ftreet, and return inftantly ! (*apart*). Adieu, fweet bridegroom, (*help-ing to get him out*) fpeed quickly back, (*looking after them*) but find Antonia gone! Dear liberty, I hail thee ! Oh Rachel, now I claim thy promife; —affift my flight, and make thy terms and fortune. Follow—follow me !   [*Exit.*

Rachel.

Rachel. I will—but let me confider firſt what I have engaged to do, to make my fortune.   Why I am to aſſiſt a pretty girl to run away from an old huſband to a young one; from age, gout, and petulance, to youth, health, and glowing love. Ay, that I will, or may I never arrive at higher honour than to attend miſſes in their bibs, and antient maidens in their ſpectacles!

End of the Fourth Act.

A C T

A C T V.

An Apartment at Don Alexis's.

A Table with Candles and Chairs.

He enters, followed by a Servant.

Alexis.

H E Y dey! why what's the meaning of all this? The family are all up, though it is paſt twelve o'clock, and my wife's apartments in a blaze—illuminated! as though it was ſome grand anniverſary. What's the meaning of all this, I ſay?

Serv. Donna Seraphina has ladies with her, Sir—they have been playing.

Alex. Playing! go, get along and let me know when they break up. (*Exit Servant.*) There's no having any reſt in this world.—No, or at leaſt not for the *huſbands* of this world.—This cuſtom of letting one's wives receive female company, is like ſhutting your gates upon the enemy, and then helping them over the wall. Not a woman but has her head full of projects, and her pockets of *billets-doux*. Well, if at laſt Don Octavio ſhould really marry my daughter, I ſhall then hope——

Enter Servant.

Serv. Don Gaſper de Frontado is without, Sir.
Alex.

Alex. Don Gasper—Don Gasper! it can't be.

Serv. He is indeed, Sir, attended by most of his servants, with drawn swords and torches.

Alex. Swords and torches—why he's mad! the near approach of matrimony has turn'd his brain. Well, no great wonder. It is Gasper sure enough! (*looking through the wing*) What a figure!—

Gasp. (*Speaking as he enters*) Bless me, why all is quiet——all is quiet, my dear nephew! ah (*looking back*) what's he gone? Not a voice in the street, but two old women quarrelling about a string of sausages.

Alex. (*Aside.*) Ay it is so—he's certainly crazy. I am very sorry Don Gasper (*gravely taking off his hat*) that any thing should have happen'd to call you from your house, at this time.

Gasp. My house—that's nothing! From my bride—from my little Tony—from the very altar, my friend. But *that* is nothing—the good of the nation must be minded. Come let us sit and to business.

Alex. As soon as you please. Zounds, what a time for him to think on the good of the nation! (*aside.*)

(*They both draw chairs, and sit looking at one another, waiting for each to begin.*)

Gasp. Be brief—my good friend, be brief!

Alex. Brief—why we hav'nt begun yet.

Gasp. Then why the devil don't we? How long am I to wait, before the mighty matter is brought upon the carpet? Do you consider that I am on the point of being married, Sir?

Alex. Pray, Sir, what would you be at?

Gasp. I be at—I want to know what you would be at.

I

Alex.

Alex. Ha, ha, ha,—why this is the ftrangeft thing! to fee an old fellow, high in the ftate, the night he fhould be married, forfake his bride, and come with a train arm'd cap-à-piè, to difturb another old fellow, and afk him what he would be at! What's your bufinefs once more?

Gafp. My bufinefs, with whom?

Alex. With me, Sir—with me! What the devil do you do here?

Gafp. That's what I want to know, Sir, and you'd beft be quick in the relation! You feem to think time of no more value to me than ftraw.

Alex. (*rifing*) Ay, ftraw—there it is! I thought he was mad; they never think of any thing but ftraw. I am forry you are thus difturbed, Don Gafper.

Gafp. (*Purfuing him*) The difturbance is no-thing, if you would but come to the point— What is the plot—Where are the confpirators, and what do they aim at?

Alex. Poor foul—poor foul! My dear friend you really fhock me very much—tho' I knew your marriage was a mad action, I did not think it would have taken effect fo foon.

Gafp. Oons! this is beyond all bearing! (*making a motion as tho' to his fword, and feems difappointed*) no fword—meet me to-morrow, Sir— meet me to-morrow!

Alex. With all my heart. By that time you'll be in a ftrait waiftcoat, and I fhall be fafe. (*Afide.*)

Gafp. I am cooler. Such old men as we are can afford to wafte no blood—but there's your ring, Sir; and let that be the laft token of good, or ill will, you ever fend me. (*Flinging the ring from him.*)

Alex.

Alex. My ring! (*taking it from the floor*) why, how came you—who gave you this ring? who gave it you?

Gasp. Why did not,—did not—oh, my mind misgives me!

Alex. You had it from your nephew—eh?

Gasp. Ye—y-e-s. (*Trembling.*)

Alex. Ha, ha, ha,—oh, a young rogue—oh, a plotting young villain! ha, ha, ha——

Gasp. What then I have—oh, shame to my years—I have been made a jest of.

Alex. A jest——Heaven grant you may be made nothing worse of! Hurry home my dear friend; you know what I said to-day about your bride's odd fancies. Hurry home, and be thankful if it *is* a jest!

Gasp. What do you imagine—do you conceive—oh, my dear, dear friend! But hold, you are in the plot——the ring is your's——you are in the plot! (*Ragefully.*)

Alex. Believe me Don Gasper——

Gasp. Oh, what a beetle, what a bat, I have been! but I'll repay your jest with interest. In the first place—and that's only for a beginning mind me, only for a beginning—— my Octavio shall never marry your daughter. How d'ye like that jest? Oh what a blind—blind—oh! (*Going off stamping.*)

Alex. (*going after him*) My dear Don Gasper, my friend, my worthy friend, I entreat—Zounds! he's gone! If it had not been for his choak-pear about Octavio, how I could laugh. Why, what the plague did that impertinent Don Julio take such a liberty with my ring for? how dared he haul me head and ears into his scheme, to laugh at his worthy uncle? But zooks it is a good laugh

after

after all—ha, ha, ha——but if Gafper now, thro'
fpite, fhould prevent Octavio's marriage! What's
to be done? hang me if I go to bed to night——
I'll find out Octavio wherever he is, make him
fteal my daughter, conclude the marriage, and then
I'll laugh with Julio, 'till my old fides crack. [*Exit.*

SCENE *changes to the Street, before* Don
Gafper's.

Enter Don Henry.

He knocks gently at the door.

Hen. I dare not be louder; but fure the ear of
love can catch the gentleft found!

Rach. (*from the balcony*) Oh, are you come,
Sir——I'll call my lady down.

Hen. Oh hafte! the minutes fly; I have fecur'd
a fafe retreat——leave all behind, and bring
Antonia only to my arms. (*A noife of people
advancing*) Hah! what noife is that? and lights
too! they come this way—furely 'tis Don Gafper's
voice——I am breathlefs with my fears.

Gafp. (*without*) Put out your lights—extinguifh
your torches, and be filent.

Hen. Ay, 'tis he—fhall I plunge this fword into
his bofom, or my own? oh, either way I'm loft!
(*Don Gafper enters, and knocks loudly.*)

Gafp. Yes, yes, I'll be a match for his great
grandfires, ring, truft me! (*Knocks again.*)

Rachel. (*from the balcony*) We are juft ready,
Sir—have a moment's patience.

Gafp. Juft ready for what? Oh I am arrived in
the very nick of fome curfed fcheme! Keep your
fwords drawn. (*to his fervants*) Come, I'll not give

5   **way**

way to fuspicions—fhe fhall have fair play—appearances may deceive.

The door opens. Antonia *enters.*

Henry. Hah! by Heaven, Antonia—we are ruin'd!

Ant. Where are you, my beft wifhes? lord of my vows, and charmer of my foul, where are you?

Henry. Oh heavens! (*half drawing his fword.*)

Gafp. Well, well, that *may* be all meant for me.

Ant. Give me your hand, my love, my life, and guide me to your bofom—the home for which I pant!

Gafp. Hum—that is rather too much, too! I'm afraid that's too fweet a morfel to be meant for my chops.

Ant. (*groping about*) Oh, are you here indeed? you frighten'd me with your filence. Here take thefe jewels, and let us hafte away.

Gafp. H-a-h, are you thereabouts, madam? (*between his teeth*) then I'm cozen'd.

Henry. (*afide*) To attempt to force her off would be in vain.

Ant. Will you not fpeak? do you repent already? before poffeffion are you cold, and falfe?

Gafp. Before——ah, ah!—well that's great comfort. Whatever is defign'd, I am beforehand with the mifchief, however.

Ant. Am I not to be your wife?—this very day did we not invoke Heaven to blefs our vows?

Gafp. Now then 'tis clearly me, and I'll be mute no longer.

Ant. Oh Henry! Henry! (*mournfully.*)

Gafp. (*ftarting*) Who doft thou take me for— Henry? Oh thou perfidious wretch!

Ant.

Ant. Don Gafper——what will become of me?
Why—why are you fo angry, Sir, at my naming
one who in the cold grave cannot rival you? I
was only going to fay, that Henry would not have
been fo unkindly filent.

Gafp. Was that all indeed, my little Tony?
but 'twas wrong to think upon a young man.
Never let your thoughts run upon a young man,
whether in a grave, or a garret.

Ant. Never, Sir, be affured. Neither in one
place, or the other, will my thoughts ever feek a
lover. But why did you not fpeak?

Gafp. Faith, you prattled love fo prettily, I
could have heard your little tongue run for ever.
But how came you out fo late, and with thefe
jewels, and parcels?

Ant. Sir!—I was—why Sir——

Rachel. Alas, Sir, we thought the city was in
arms, and pack'd up our things to fecure 'em.
Lord, Sir, we were fo fcared! about plots, and
robberies, and—

Ant. Yes, Sir, terrified to death.

Gafp. Oh it's all quell'd now—'tis all over, my
pretty chuck. As foon as *I* appear'd amongft 'em,
and threaten'd 'em, and harangued 'em on their
duty, they were as filent as the foft tread of a
thief on a dark ftair-cafe. I am refolv'd fhe fhan't
know what a gull I was. (*afide*) Come now let's
in, and join our tender hearts in one.

Ant. Pardon me, Sir. Day is on the point of
breaking—dear welcome day! and I am refolv'd
to pafs it unbound by any vows, but thofe of love.

Gafp. How!

Ant. In this one point, Sir, I muft govern, or
here I vow moft folemnly, never to be yours.

Gafp.

Gasp. Oh its a rash vow—a most unjustifiable vow!

Rach. Not so rash a vow as that you want her to make.

Gasp. What's that, minx?

Rach. Why Sir, with submission, I say its most rash and unjustifiable, for eighteen to rise out of bed, and go to church, to vow to love sixty-five—and I'll maintain it.

Gasp. But the vow was made, hussey, and all vows must be kept—religiously kept! and therefore, though it goes against me, even this last shall be kept. So come in, my little Tony, and learn of your nown Hubby, never to break a vow.

(*all go in.*)

Henry. That secures me! Her delicacy is safe from insult, and when I see her next, it shall be with powers to suppress his audacious, fancied rights, and close the necessity for these degrading acts for ever. [*Exit.*

S C E N E *changes to* **Don Alexis's Garden.**

He enters, leading in Octavio.

Alex. Gad I am glad I found ye—'twas devilish lucky! Viola is certainly somewhere in the garden—both my wife and Carlota assured me that she was.

Octav. And the ladder of ropes is suspended from the place you pointed out.

Alex. Exactly there—I help'd to fix it myself—'tis very secure.

Octav. The dear little madcap must have her way; but 'tis strange she prefers scaling a wall at midnight, to walking quietly thro' the gate in the sunshine. Hist!—I hear the tread of gentle feet.

Alex.

Alex. Then I'm off. If ſhe ſhould find us together, the perverſe baggage would ſuſpeɛt our
intelligence, and that would ſpoil all——ſo I'm
off! *(lowering his voice.)*   [*Exit.*

Oɛtav. In a few hours, expeɛt us at your feet
aſking pardon and bleſſing. *(A pauſe.)* Charming
Viola, appear! I hear you not; yet by the ſoft
influence about me, I am ſure you are near.
What delightful faculty is this, which allows us to
be conſcious of the preſence of the objeɛt we adore,
without the vulgar intervention of the ſenſes ?—
It muſt be the privilege of pureſt love !

Seraph. *(entering.)* The privilege of fancy——
all mere fancy; tho' you would'exalt it into a
faculty !

Oɛtav. Hab, my charmer ! *(catching her in his
arms)* faculties, and fancies, are now equally nothing;——all loſt in tranſport, at finding thee in
my arms.

Seraph. I proteſt I begin to believe you very
dangerous. I infiſt on your quitting me this in-
ſtant. *(breaking from him)* Heavens what a ſitua-
tion ! in the arms of a man—alone—in a garden,
at two o'clock in the morning ? *(Aſide.)*

Oɛtav. What doſt think of, ſweet angel ?

Seraph.. That the ſooner we are out of this
place the better.

Oɛtav. *(Aſide.)* Suppoſe I ſecure her mine ! I
almoſt fear ſome new caprice——and if I miſtake
not, her little heart flutters at this moment, in
uniſon with my own. Dear bewitching woman,
let me once more taſte——

Seraph. Hold, Sir! or by all that's good——
(breaking from him) I never knew till now what
reſiſtance meant. *(Aſide.)*

                                              Oɛtav.

Octav. By heavens I will not lose this charm-ing moment!

Seraph. Then you lose me for ever—make your election!

Octav. This moment is presented to us by love —let us prove ourselves worthy of the boon!

Seraph. How? by *disgracing* love?

Octav. We'll argue that point hereafter; but now————

Seraph. Hold, Sir—I am neither blind to your intention, nor to my own danger—but know you are meditating an irremediable crime!

Octav. How irremediable? Love itself shall re-medy the crimes it makes.

Seraph. Hah! you know not what you speak of, nor can I explain myself—but let us fly!

Octav. Then we *will* fly my little trembler, and Hymen shall————

Seraph. Yet stay—I cannot go with you alone —you must consent that a lady accompanies us.

Octav. Who?

Seraph. No matter. You must promise me, without asking questions, to conduct *her* safely to Don Sebastian; and then to conduct me in safety to your father's.

Octav. To my ghostly father you mean—to a priest?

Seraph. No, to Don Gasper—on those terms I scale the wall with you, and on no other.

Octav. It is odd, and mysterious; but I'll scale walls with you on any terms. Where is the lady?

Seraph. We shall find her in the next walk— oh, no, she is hast'ning hither. (*Enter* Viola, *veil'd.*) Come fair damsel, this is the valourous knight who is to conduct us thro' all the inter-vening dragons, and giants, to the quiet and sober

K   pale

pale of matrimony—where we fhall grow good, and ftupid : (*drawling*) and recollect the kind action of this night, with matronly thankfulnefs and decency.

Octav. (*Afide.*) 'Tis a vile thought, and fticks moft indigeftibly! Why muft love be thus fhackled? I feel I fhall repent, and leap the pale;—but I am fairly caught now, and muft fubmit. Come my little fawns! take each an arm.——Egad, let us make hafte, or fome unlucky ideas, which are growing rather ponderous, will prevent my flight over the wall!

Seraph. I'll be hang'd if it is not the idea of matrimony you find fo heavy!—but be of good comfort, Signor, and make fpeed—your fate has prepared a confolation you little expect. [*Exeunt.*

SCENE, Don Gafper's. *He enters.*

Gafp. Well, day at laft is broad awake; and the vile night, which cloaks fo many fchemes, and villainous plots, againft the peace of wary hufbands, is pafs'd away—and all hath gone well! yes, all hath gone well, except with my poor aching bones, and fleeplefs eyes.   Spent all thefe hours upon a mat at Antonia's chamber door—dared not leave it.   Truly fhe is a treafure, but if to fecure it I muft fag out the remnant of my life in thefe a-larms, and fears, and mifgivings.——Well, well, 'tis too late now to think about that; my hour is come! (*Dolefully.*)

Enter a Servant.

Serv. Don Octavio, and a lady, Sir.   [*Exit.*
      [*Octavio enters, leading Seraphina, veil'd.*
Octav. Permit me, Sir, to afk your protection
                                        for

for this lady for a few hours;—if you knew her, you would think fhe had a right to claim it.

Gafp. To claim it—why, who is fhe?

Octav. That I am forbid to tell—do you re- leafe me from my promife, madam?

Seraph. No, certainly;—and yet if I did, it were much the fame thing, for you do not know me.

Gafp. Not know the lady!

Seraph. Believe me he does not; and yet if you afk him, he'll fwear he does.

Octav. Surely, tho' you are veil'd, I can fwear you are the fame fweet melting creature, who in a certain garden————

Seraph. Found herfelf in your arms; and after- wards leapt the wall with you—that you may fafely fwear.

Octav. Yet I know you not—ha, ha, ha, per- mit me *(apart)*————Perhaps you'll deny being her, whom I am to marry to day?

Seraph. Oh, no—I fwear I will marry you to day, if Don Alexis gives confent.

Octav. We have more than his confent—his ardent wifhes.

Seraph. Yet I fhall not be your's.

Octav. Why, what a fweet enigmatical charmer you are!

Seraph. *(to Don Gafper)* If I miftake not, Sir, this houfe has a miftrefs—may I be permitted to wait on Donna Antonia?

Gafp. Madam—ma—Octavio! *(Whifpers.)*

Octav. Oh yes, of rank and reputation—but a little capricious.

Gafp. Pardon me, madam! I will wait on you

to Antonia's apartment.——I fhan't care to leave them together tho'! (*Afide.*)

     [*Exit, leading Seraphina.*

Octav. What can fhe mean with her riddle-merees? I am perplex'd (*Sebaftian enters with Viola.*) Hah Don Sebaftian! What the weighty ceremony fo lightly over? Madam, I wifh you all the joys which belong to your new ftate. Dear Sebaftian (*taking him afide*) tell me—how doft feel?

Sebaf. Feel!

Octav. Ay;—in a few hours I fhall be in the fame clafs, and I want to guefs how it is.

Sebaf. If you love as I do, you'll feel as I do—bleft!

Octav. I fear all you married rogues are fo many decoy ducks; you look up with envy, and cry *quake, quake,* to your fellows at large; and when you have coax'd us into the fnare, clap your wings, and exult.

Viola. (*running to Sebaftian.*) Oh, I hear my father's voice—I would not have him fee you at this inftant. (*Apart.*) Pardon my freedom Don Octavio, but it will be infinitely kind if you'll both leave me.

Sebaf. Thofe fears are idle my charmer—the moment *muft* arrive.

Viola. Nay, do not ftay-to argue, but oblige me!

Octav. What, Sir, fo much of a hufband in half an hour, as to difpute a command? I'll take him to tafk, madam, and give him a leffon on obedience.   [*Exeunt.*

Alexis. (*without*) Octavio, and a lady veil'd? (*entering*) then all is right! Hah Viola! well, tell me, is it all over—are you married?

Viola. Yes, Sir.

           Alex.

Alex. Yes, Sir—enough faid! ha, ha, ha,—now I can laugh at Gafper, and enjoy Don Julio's joke—ha, ha, ha——and you too—you have been finely nick'd—I have been oblig'd to cheat you into marrying the man you liked—ha, ha, ha——

Viola. Oh, Sir, forgive what I have done!

Alex. Forgive thee, my girl! ay that I will— here's my hand upon't.—Hah Don Gafper! (*he enters*) your moft obedient very humble fervant! How do you find yourfelf after your laft night's whim, Sir?—My feal-ring is at your fervice, at any time, Don Gafper—ha, ha, ha,—two jokes at once—I fhall laugh now, 'till I am a grand-father.

Gafp. If you laugh till my Octavio makes you a grandfather, it will be a very long fit I pro-mife ye.

Alex. D'ye think fo? I'll truft him!

Gafp. He is now in the next room, at the feet of a young lady, whofe charms are fufficient, I truft, to blot thofe of your daughter from his heart.

Alex. What's that? Octavio at the feet of a lady! d'ye hear that, Viola?

Gafp. Your daughter—Pardon me, fair lady!

Alex. Ay, Sir, and your daughter too—your daughter! Let me fee you encourage her huf-band to kneel to other women in your houfe.

Gafp. Her hufband—ha, ha, ha.

Alex. Zounds, Sir, this is no laughing matter —how dare you, Sir—Why, Viola, why don't you rave and ftorm, as women do on thefe occa-fions?

Viola. Alas, Sir! I have no right.

Alex. No right! I fhall fee that. Here Don Octavio, I fay! The very day of his marriage— nay within the hour!   (*Enter Octavio.*)

Octav.

Octav. Don Alexis—your pleafure?

Alex. My pleafure, Sir, is, that—Zounds!—
that *your* pleafure fhall be with my daughter.

Octav. 'Tis very kind—nothing can make me
fo happy.

Alex. Then what the devil do you mean by—
by—your father fays you were at the feet of a lady.

Octav. I was.

Alex. You was!

Octav. Why fhould that offend you? Do you
not wifh me to love your daughter?

Alex. Love my daughter, and kneel to another!

Octav. All miftake, Sir—another! I'll convince you that Viola alone (*going to the wing*)
here fhe comes! the dear lively girl! who leapt
a garden wall, to give a fober marriage the air
of a romance.

Alex. Oons! where am I? are not you my
daughter? (*twitching off* Viola's *veil*) yes. Did
you not leap the wall with him?

Viola. Yes, Sir.

Alex. And are you not married?

Viola. I am indeed! (*curtfeying.*)

Alex. And did you, Madam, leap a wall?

Seraph. Yes, Sir.

Alex. And are you married too?

Seraph. I am, indeed! (*throws up her veil, and
curtfeys.*)

Alex. My wife—Oons—my wife!

Octav. Amazement! his wife!

Gafp. His wife leap the wall with my Octavio
—ha, ha, ha. I'll add another five hundred moidores to your yearly allowance, for that my boy!
Prithee, dear Don, indulge your laugh; you were
in a very fine vein a minute ago—ha, ha, ha—
now laugh till you're a grandfather!

I   *Seraph.*

Seraph. Don Octavio, I have used you ill; but I truft your generofity will pardon my taking advantage of your partiality for me, to ferve two amiable and faithful lovers.

Octav. You have ufed me ill, indeed! yet hang it, come, I am not married—I am not married however! (*afide*) Yes, Madam, I can forgive *you*; but how fhall I forgive myfelf? I had you—oh, diftraction! I had you alone—amidft the confcious fhades of night—and in my power!

Seraph. Pardon me, Sir! no woman can be alone, nor in the power of any man, whilft fhe refpects herfelf, and is guarded by a fenfe of her duty. You fee, Don Alexis, what benefits arife from plotting *without* a woman. Ha, ha, ha.

Alex. Oh, I fhall be mad! fo it was my wife, then, to whom you were kneeling? and it was you whom I prefs'd yefterday to grant him fome fmall favours?

Seraph. Juft fo, my fweet Hubby!

Alex. Oh!

Gafp. Come, be merry, old Gentleman.—A companion for your feal ring—two jokes at once, ha, ha, ha.

Alex. Ay, you have it all to nothing now. And you have the impudence to love my wife? (*to Octavio.*)

Octav. More than ever, now there's no danger of matrimony.

Alex. And you are now confidering when you fhall make me a—a fatyr, eh? come, be frank— when is it to be?

Octav. Faith, I wifh I could tell.

Seraph. I will anfwer for him!—it fhall be *never*; whilft you repofe a generous confidence in me, and allow me to be the guardian of my own honour. (*Don Gafp. goes out.*)

Octav.

Octav. Now I intreat you, my dear Don Alexis, be a very tyrant! suspect her, watch her, and confine her—will you be so much my friend?

Alex. I don't know what I shall be yet;—both as husband and father, I have ingeniously contrived to bite myself most d—n—bly! As for you, Madam, (*to* Viola) bread and water, and a dark chamber, shall be your lot————

Sebas. (*entering*) No, Sir,—*I* am the arbiter of her lot;—however, I confirm half your punishment; and a dark chamber she shall certainly have *.

Alex. What then, thou art really married—and married to Sebastian!

Viola. Dear, Sir, you assured me, that of the two fools you preferred *him*.

Alex. Yes, but I depended on your perverse-ness, hussey?

Gasp. (*Leading in* Antonia) Come, you, who have not seen my little pet, behold her—Nay, I present her to ye all, as the pattern of meekness and perfect love—Oh its a sweet pudsey.

Ant. Meekness, alas! you should not answer for; you know I am a woman.   My perfect love, indeed you may—the world has not a heart so truly wedded as Antonia's—behold its master—its lawful lord, my husband! (*Pointing to the opposite door.*)

Don Henry. (*entering*) Come, my Antonia, to his arms! Yes, I *am* thy husband—now I stand boldly forward, and proclaim my title—I am thy husband! that dear distinction which heaven has blest me with, heaven only shall reclaim!

Octav. What! am I to lose my mother as well as my wife?

* This is the expression, I am told, which had nearly prov'd fatal to the Comedy. I should not have printed it, but from the resolution I have religiously kept, of restoring every thing that was objected to.   *Alex.*

Alex. (*To Gasp.*) Your nephew! why is this full moon? We are all going to run out of our wits.

Seraph. Don't be dishearten'd—tho' it should be so—*You'll* not have far to run!

Gasp. Why Julio, what in the name of——

Henry. No, Sir—not Julio, but Don Henry. That Don Henry whom you so basely reported to be dead; that you might dishonour him in security.

Gasp. How!—why—why you *are* dead—as good as dead; you are dead in law—you are outlaw'd, banish'd——

Henry. No, Sir, neither——restored to my country! Behold my pardon! (*Shews a paper.*)

Gasp. Your pardon!—hum! Now, then I see the whole;—I must be telling my secrets, with a devil to it! Well you got it through me you know—you may thank the music of my moidores for that dance!

Henry. No, Sir! (*throwing down a purse*) there is the gold you basely barter'd for the pardon you solicited. *My* pardon I obtain'd from the hands of majesty itself—from our gracious queen! Oh, when her kingdom's foes provoke correction from her subjects arms, then shall my sword again be drawn, nor ask forgiveness for its ardent duty!

Gasp. Well, very well—but what has your pardon to do with my wife? (*putting her behind him*) What have you to do with Tony?

Henry. She is *my* wife; made mine by contract, before you destin'd her the bliss of being your's. Pardon me then, my sweet Antonia! (*taking her from Gasper*) if I deprive you of this venerable charmer, and give you in his place a husband!

L

Alex.

Alex. Hum! hum! (*Sings.*)

> Once I was a merry old man,
> But now the cafe is chang'd!

Who could have thought that my old feal ring would ever have been a talifman to make lovers happy, and fave a Greybeard from folly?

Seraph. Come Don Gafper, let me advife you to think your lofs a gain—you fee in your humble fervant, what mifchievous creatures young wives are;—fhe'd plague your heart out, as I do my old hufband's.

Alex. Faith fhe fays true. A minute ago I thought the laugh on my fide; but 'tis ftill on your own. You have loft a young wife, and I have found one.

Gafp. Why, to fay truth, if it were not that at prefent I feel a little aukward, and don't know very well which way to look.—As to your contract I might perhaps difpute its powers, but as here is a ftroke or two of mine, which may be, I fhan't be forry to have drop'd, e'en go to church i'gad's name; and when ye come home beware of plots and feal rings!

Ant. This is generous! The fentiments you profefs'd for me I fee will be converted to a more decent regard, and we fhall all be united in the bands of charming friendfhip.

Alex. Gad this looks like a fort of general amnefty—fo let the frolick go round! But dare my faults hope forgivenefs here? (*to the houfe*) Yes;—I am on this fpot an old offender; and have fo often gratefully experienced the candour of my judges, that I truft now to meet their pardon—and invoke the gracious fign!

F I N I S.

EPILOGUE,

By Mr. COBB.

SPOKEN BY MISS FARREN.

A Mourning Bride!—that wou'd be fomething new—
(That I'm a Mourning Hufband is too true,
Cries old Sir Tefty in his gouty chair,)
" Ah could I wedlock's fatal flip repair !
" But young wives are a fort of flying gout,
" Torments for which no cure was e'er found out;
" Both old men's plagues, to punifh youthful tricks,
" Equally difficult, I fear, to fix.
" Of wife and gout alike I ftand in dread,
" For both, alas ! fometimes affect the head."
   Thus rail old cynics, ftriving to difparage
The charming filken ties of modern marriage.
In former times, when folks agreed to wed,
The filent bride by filent bridegroom led,
Up to the altar march'd in folemn ftate,
All was demure, and ftupidly fedate.
Imprefs'd with awe, while neither dar'd to fpeak,
A wedding was a mere Ballet Tragique.
Thank Heav'n we're paft the ages of romance ;
Wedlock is now a kind of country dance,
Where man and wife with fmiles each other greet,
Take hands, change fides, and part as foon as meet;
Pleafure's foft accents ev'ry care difpel,
While Hymen fiddles Vive la Bagatelle.
Bleft age ! when ceremony's chains are worn,
Like bracelets, not to fetter, but adorn.
When we affume deep mourning's fable fhew,
'Tis etiquette prefcribes the form of woe :
Whate'er our lofs, we muft have fafhion's leave,
Ere we can venture decently to grieve.

                                    Blamelefs

EPILOGUE.

Blameless the heir, o'er the dear parchment chuckles,
If he's unpowder'd, and puts on black buckles,
Till the grey frock speaks his first anguish o'er,
And he's but half as wretched as before.
Ere the gay widow first abroad is seen,
Deck'd in exhilarating bombazeen,
While the dear Col'nel visits unsuspected,
And she's as well as could have been expected;
Custom's indulgence wisely does she borrow,
In cards of compliments exhausts her sorrow;
Of tears her black-edg'd paper fills the place,
Mourns as her proxy, and preserves her face.
Our Mourning Bride, who with no sorrow labours,
And mourns but in *appearance,* like her neighbours,
Tho' forc'd by etiquette, good humour loves, as well
    as any here;
Blest in the fate which these kind smiles decree her,
She hopes her friends will often come to see her.

The following NEW PIECES, *written by Mrs.* COWLEY,
  may be had of Messrs. ROBINSON, *Pater-noster-Row.*

1. The RUNAWAY, a Comedy, Price 1s. 6d.
2. ALBINA, a Tragedy, 1s. 6d.
3. WHO'S THE DUPE? a Farce, 1s.
4. BELLE'S STRATAGEM, a Comedy, 1s. 6d.
5. WHICH IS THE MAN? a Comedy, 1s. 6d.
6. BOLD STROKE FOR A HUSBAND, a Comedy, 1s. 6d.
7. MORE WAYS THAN ONE, a Comedy, 1s. 6d.
8. First Part of THE MAID OF ARRAGON, a Poem, 4to.
2s. 6d.
9. The SCOTTISH VILLAGE, a Poem, 4to. 2s.

www.ingramcontent.com/pod-product-compliance
Lightning Source LLC
Chambersburg PA
CBHW020048030726
47499CB00007B/2637